"I don't like games, Mrs. Cameron."

Abbie could believe that. Sean Baldwin's blue-black eyes were as steady as the gun at his side. He'd probably never played a game in his life.

She wanted to tell him she wasn't really Mrs. Cameron...because keeping up so many charades was like juggling hand grenades. One of them was sure to slip and explode. She'd already slipped twice, and he'd noticed.

"Your last bodyguard got shot to smithereens in your stead," Sean continued. "Do you remember that? Do you remember how he died?"

Abbie took a deep breath and met the dark, angry eyes of the dead bodyguard's replacement.

"I'm not going to leave your side for a second," he said. "So, try to remember what's at stake, Mrs. Cameron. Someone out there wants you dead."

Dear Reader,

Sometime, somewhere, any woman might need protection. And who could be more sexy—or dangerous—than her bodyguard? You're about to meet some of the bodyguards at Protection Enterprises, Incorporated. Last month we were pleased to bring you *Guarded Moments*, the first book in the MY BODYGUARD miniseries.

This month Carly Bishop brings you *Shadow Lover*. Bodyguard Sean Baldwin has never lost a client...but then, he's never fallen head over heels in love with one, either.

I know you'll enjoy *Shadow Lover*, and I hope you'll look for the next MY BODYGUARD title: #398 *Protect Me, Love* by Alice Orr. Don't miss the MY BODYGUARD miniseries!

Sincerely,

Debra Matteucci
Senior Editor and Editorial Coordinator
Harlequin Books
300 East 42nd Street
New York, NY 10017

Shadow Lover
Carly Bishop

Harlequin Books

TORONTO • NEW YORK • LONDON
AMSTERDAM • PARIS • SYDNEY • HAMBURG
STOCKHOLM • ATHENS • TOKYO • MILAN
MADRID • WARSAW • BUDAPEST • AUCKLAND

To Sarah
the brightest star in my firmament.

ISBN 0-373-22394-3

SHADOW LOVER

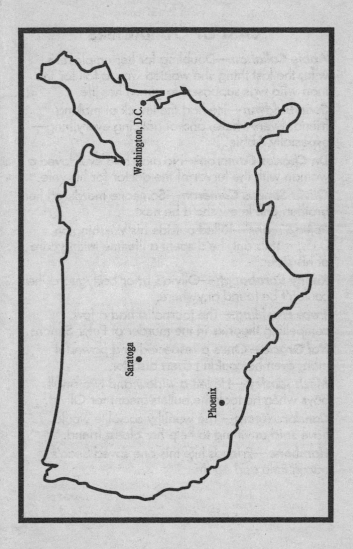

Washington, D.C.

Saratoga

Phoenix

CAST OF CHARACTERS

Abbie Callahan—Doubling for her employer's wife, the last thing she wanted was to fall for the man who was supposed to guard her life.

Sean Baldwin—He had the knack of making friends everywhere, and of noticing everything—especially Abbie.

Dr. Charles Cameron—No man had ever loved a woman with the fervor of the doctor for his wife.

Olivia Simons Cameron—Someone murdered her brother. She knew she'd be next.

Peter Simons—Killed outside his Washington, D.C., restaurant, he'd spent a lifetime taking care of his sister.

Kenny Rorabaugh—Olivia's prior bodyguard, he couldn't be found anywhere.

Trace Freehling—The journalist had a few compelling theories in the murder of Peter Simons.

Hal Gracie—Once a respected and powerful man, even he couldn't avert disaster.

Mitch Tensley—He left a widow and two small boys when he took the bullets meant for Olivia.

Candace Kemp—The wealthy socialite would have said anything to help her oldest friend.

Hambone—Friends like this one saved Sean's bacon time and again.

Prologue

August

Charles Langston Cameron III turned a weary glance on the ornate antique clock that graced his desk. He couldn't seem to concentrate, to hold his attention to the meandering, fearful, even incoherent narration of his patient. Her dreams, the dreams of a woman high in the power hierarchy of the state department, disturbed him, set his own psyche on edge. He could not even listen to her had he not been given the highest security clearances by the FBI. Nevertheless, her fears, her private demons, evoked Cameron's own and he felt his middle-aged body squirm.

What troubled him most was not that he would hear some terrible secret or some piece of information on which the fate of the free world rested. He treated such information as he would the penny-ante secrets of a homeless D.C. vagrant drunk—with the utmost discretion. What gnawed at the edges of his mind was that the political and international power of this woman—and ten or fifteen others like her in his psychiatric practice—that such awesome power provided no insulation, proffered no guarantee, bestowed no assurance of any control over life itself, or even one's own soul.

Cameron's name was an affectation. Born the illegitimate son of a deflowered, disinherited debutante, he bore the names that belonged to other old, moneyed, powerful Maryland families, the ones his mother most admired. But Cameron had taken life into his own hands early on.

He had pulled himself up from the muck and disgrace by nothing but his own willpower to become one of the foremost psychiatrists on the eastern seaboard. His fame and reputation and celebrity exceeded even his own wildest dreams.

He walked among the wealthy and privileged as an equal. He owned free and clear an estate in Maryland as elegant and refined as any. And he had wooed and won a national treasure, the beautiful daughter of Avery Simons, an elder statesman without peer.

Olivia was his.

But in his heart of hearts, triggered by the psychic wounds and the echoes of childhood fears of the politically powerful patient sitting before him now, Charles Langston Cameron III feared he would lose it all.

He commanded a hundred thousand dollars per engagement on the lecture circuit, from baccalaureate addresses at the most prestigious Ivy League universities to keynote addresses at exclusive writers' seminars. He restored equilibrium, even sanity, to the most powerful men and women in the nation. Having Olivia Simons Cameron at his side and in his bed made him weak in the knees with gratitude and humility and pride.

Like any other couple, he and Liv had their problems, but he had no real reason to believe that they would not all be resolved, or that he would lose it all. Still, the fear that had risen in him triggered such a deep-seated alarm that he could hardly manage to conceal his upheaval from his patient.

He knew such fears arose from a deep subconscious knowing. A part of him knew the Truth with a capital T. Unless he acted with the utmost care, with the highest regard for the universe and the deepest humility, he *would* lose it all.

But he could not see how.

His patient daubed at her tears with an exquisitely embroidered linen handkerchief. "What must I do, Dr. Cameron?" she cried. "What can I do?"

He skewered up his courage and responded to her pain from a deeply empathetic compassion. He knew her fear. Her fear was inside him in another shape. Maybe it was only her fear contaminating him. With all the skill of his profession, he led her to the point of seeing for herself the meaning of her dreams. By that time, the gold-plated clock hands reached four-forty. He rose and helped her from her chair. "Protect yourself, my dear," he urged her. "Sacrifice your sleepwalking. Wake up and mark your territory and protect your soul. You must simply begin."

Acceptance dawned in her teary eyes, and she nodded, then gathered together her belongings and departed.

Cameron lost no time in leaving for the afternoon himself. He called down to have his car brought around, let himself out his private door, took the VIP elevator to the VIP parking level, and slid into the rich, leather-upholstered driver's seat of his Mercedes sedan. He forgot to notice which valet had waited upon him, which troubled him.

He treated everyone—even those who served him—with uncommon respect. He must be more upset than he knew. He wanted to get home to Olivia and prayed she would be there and not out on one of her charity functions. Heading toward his Maryland estate, he suffered the choking mid-August Washington, D.C., rush-hour traffic. He was just reaching to insert a calming CD into the player when his pager activated itself. He plucked the vibrating lump from his belt and checked the LCD.

He recognized the switchboard number of the Georgetown University Medical Center. His brow creased. He had no patients hospitalized, certainly none there. Negotiating a tortuously slow access off the Capital Beltway, he lifted his car phone from its cradle and punched in the hospital number.

The switchboard put him on hold. The next voice he heard was the voice of doom his unconscious had sensed in the midst of the session with his last patient. "Dr. Cameron, your wife was brought in an hour ago, hemorrhaging. She's in surgery now."

His heart went cold as stone. His head throbbed so painfully that he felt as though he were having a stroke. He pulled out of the traffic snarl and bulled his way down the emergency access lane and sped cross-town to the medical center where his beloved Olivia might already have bled to death.

He couldn't imagine what must have hap-pened...an accident, a car crash... He dared not imagine what else. He abandoned his Mercedes in the hospital drive and tore through the maze of hallways and clinics and wards to the surgical suites.

Inside, the surgeon rose from her chair and introduced herself when she recognized him. He knew her to be one of the city's premier gynecological surgeons.

His heart seemed to stop.

"Dr. Cameron. I'm so sorry to meet you under such conditions."

"What—" he choked.

"The surgery went as well as could be expected. Your wife is a fighter. She'll recover, I'm quite certain. Dr. Cameron...I'm terribly sorry for your loss."

Confusion rankled through his overpowering relief. What loss? He scraped a hand through his thick head of hair. "You just said she would recover—"

He broke off. The weary surgeon looked at him with a terrible compassion reserved for good news, bad news pronouncements. "For the baby, Dr. Cameron...Olivia miscarried."

The baby. Dear God. Pain of a loss he hadn't even imagined poured through him like thick scalding tar. *The baby.* His deepest desire mocking him.

Outwardly, Charles Langston Cameron III took the news like a man. But in his soul he crumpled to his knees in the surgeon's lounge of the university medical complex and howled.

Chapter One

November

"A matter of life and death, you said." Abbie Callahan stroked a wrinkle from her gray wool skirt though the effort hardly mattered. Rushing from San Diego to La Guardia to downtown Manhattan without pause left her feeling more rumpled than her clothes. "What did you mean?"

Delia Barry blinked at Abbie from across her desk in an office high above the fray in midtown Manhattan. The offices, Abbie knew, served as the headquarters of a high-end bodyguard agency, Protection Services, Inc. Delia Barry apparently handled the day-to-day operation of the office, and the only thing Abbie knew aside from that was that even to enter the door meant signing your life away in blood to keep secret what went on here.

"Abbie...may I call you Abbie?"

"Of course. Please. Go on."

Delia tilted her head. "Do you know who Charles Langston Cameron III is?"

An unexpected interest rippled through Abbie. "Yes, I do. Who doesn't?"

"Tell me what you know of him."

"He's a D.C. psychiatrist, mentor to the powers that be. State department, Senate and House patients. It's rumored he's even been called to counsel the First Lady." Delia nodded, inviting more. Abbie went on. "Cameron is married to Olivia Simons. He leads life in the public eye but has managed never to compromise the identity of his high-profile patients. He's brilliant. Wealthy in his own right, flamboyant in an understated way."

"And you admire him professionally?"

"Very much."

"Why?"

Abbie didn't even have to think why. "I met him once—at a conference in San Francisco where he spoke. He inspires trust. He demands honesty and gives it. He knows what darkness is in us all, and he shares what he knows. He deals in reality and peels away layers of illusion with more grace than I've ever seen anywhere else. He has a wonderful sense of poetic justice. He's..." Abbie broke off and smiled. "I'm making Cameron sound like the voice in the wilderness, aren't I?"

Delia responded without expression. "Yes. But it may be true." She hesitated briefly, then went on to another subject. "Do you have as high a regard for Olivia Cameron?"

"I've never met her, but I know she's deeply committed to lost and stolen children—among several important charities."

Delia nodded. "Olivia's brother, Peter Simons, was murdered several weeks ago. Do you remember seeing it in the news?"

"Yes. It was the talk of the San Diego Police Department at the time."

A crease marred Delia's lovely brow. "I'm not sure I understand your connection with the San Diego P.D."

"I'd been consulting, sort of, on a murder case there—à la 'Murder She Wrote,'" Abbie joked.

Her day job was as a story analyst for a couple of the major film studios, but a few years ago she'd called in a tip on a lark to the S.D.P.D. "I was fooling around with what I had gleaned from news reports in a high-profile murder case—just like I would if I were trouble-shooting a script," Abbie explained. "I came up with what seemed to me to be the motive of who I believed was the real murderer." She shrugged. The joke among the homicide squad was "Call Abbie" in the vein of the *Ghostbusters*'s "Who you gonna call?" She'd become their unofficial means-and-motive guru. "Anyway, I turned out to be right. I've sat around with the detectives there, brainstorming on a couple of other capital cases since then."

"And you've been successful?" Delia asked.

Abbie nodded. "It's just this odd talent I have, to see the bigger picture and the key details at once. Nothing special."

"Get a clue, Abbie," Delia answered sharply. "Don't even *think* that way. It sounds to me as if you did what the police and prosecutors combined—all the king's horses and all the king's men—couldn't do. It makes me crazy that women don't know their own value—or ask for it, either. The police pay low-life informers. Have they paid you?"

Abbie shrugged. "There are the usual rewards for information leading to arrests and convictions. I've always funneled them back into charities." Delia said nothing, but her expression put Abbie on the defensive. "I know what it is to grow up without a dad, that's all." She took a deep breath. "They've never arrested anyone in connection with Peter Simons's murder, have they?"

"No—"

"Does this life and death thing you called me here to discuss have to do with his murder?"

Delia gave a brief shake of her head. "Not really." She paused. "Abbie, what I'm about to tell you now must be kept in the strictest confidence. Protection Services can only offer the kind of discretion and safeguards necessary to its clientele with an absolute guarantee of secrecy."

Abbie nodded, but without understanding where she fit in. "I don't know how I can help you."

"You will." Delia's chin raised. "So, I have your word that you will never breach the confidences I give you now?"

"Yes—but you must understand I need to reserve judgment as to whether I can be of any help."

Delia inclined her head, then rose from her seat behind the modest desk. "Let's go for a walk."

She retrieved a coat from a coat tree tucked discreetly in a corner of her office. Abbie rose and put on her coat, as well. She followed Delia Barry into the elevator, which descended to street level without stopping. Pushing through the revolving door, Abbie pulled the black lamb's wool collar up around her neck against the slicing cold wind of a particularly brutal November day in Manhattan.

After several blocks, Delia picked up where she had left off. "Every generation of Olivia's family has suffered real tragedy. When Olivia and Peter were small children, Ambassador Simons and his wife lost two other children in childbirth. Then Olivia's mother succumbed to some exotic disease she picked up in the Far East where the ambassador was on assignment. The very next month, Ambassador Simons's brother, who was then the odds-on pick for the Democratic presidential nomination, died in a plane crash."

Abbie's heart cringed at Delia's recounting. Only the Kennedys were more well known for the tragedies in their family.

Delia went on. "The tragedies have begun to strike the family again." Apparently, Olivia had suffered a miscarriage only days before her brother Peter was murdered. Then the threats against Olivia's life began. "Ambassador Simons was roughed up by an intruder on his estate. He had a massive stroke as a result—but in all of that, only Peter Simons's murder had made the national news."

Abbie's first instinct was to dive in and help in whatever way she could, but she'd been trying, lately, to temper her leaps into the unknown, to try to take a little less on faith.

Blind faith had gotten her into any number of emotional scrapes. She would hear Delia out, but Abbie promised herself to walk away and think about whatever was asked of her before she plunged ahead.

"If I'm correct," she said, "that Protection Services, Inc. is primarily a bodyguard service, I have to tell you, everything I know about bodyguards I learned from movies. How can I possibly help?"

Skirting a couple of in-line skaters, Delia shrugged. "None of that matters. Charles Cameron is looking for a double for his wife."

"A double? Me?"

"You." Delia nodded grimly and turned in to the doors to the Paramount Hotel. A doorman assisted and asked how he could help, but Delia knew where she was going. Abbie gawked at the stark furnishings and starker lines in harsh battleship grays, the hip, retro, quintessentially—for all she knew—New York hotel lobby.

Feeling very much like a fish out of water, an intruder into a vaguely dark and tongue-in-cheek-sinister scene, Abbie felt a flush of excitement and stood rooted to the slate-colored floor to ground herself. Impatiently, Delia pulled Abbie along to the left into what seemed fearfully small elevators to her.

In the cocoon of the elevator cage, Delia spoke softly. "Protection Services is not in the business of providing for such unusual requests. Charles Cameron, however, is a long-standing client with...special needs."

Distracted by the environs of the hotel, Abbie had lost track of Delia's stunning revelation that Charles Cameron was seeking a double for his wife. It took Abbie until the elevator doors opened again to realize that she was about to meet Charles Cameron again, this time not as an admirer, but as a candidate for the role of a double for his wife.

And by then, they stood outside the door of the suite in which Cameron himself awaited them.

He greeted Delia briefly, then turned the full measure of his attention on Abbie. She knew photographs of the man never did his vitality or charisma any justice. Nearing fifty years old, he was not an attractive man, but people wound up forgetting that when faced with the sheer magnetic force of his personality.

He trained all that amazing focus on Abbie, taking in her flighty white-blond hair, the color of her eyes, the shape of her body as he assisted her out of her coat.

His scrutiny embarrassed her. How ridiculous that she should be here interviewing for understudy to the role of the grown daughter of a world-renowned ambassador, Cameron's stunningly beautiful wife, Olivia Simons...

Cameron tossed her coat onto the back of a black minimalist chair. "Memory served me well," he said at last.

"I'm flattered that you remember me at all, Dr. Cameron."

"Perhaps I wouldn't have," he admitted, "had I been less taken by your resemblance to Olivia. But that's not the whole truth. *I* was flattered," he went on, "that as a Hollywood story analyst, you came to my presentation armed with far more insightful questions into the human condition than most of my colleagues. But then, character and motivation are the essence of fine drama, are they not?"

"They are. Thank you."

He surveyed her up and down once more, then took her hands, examining them as a piano maestro might inspect the hands of a potential student. "This... transformation will take some work," he muttered thoughtfully. "But with a little attention to the details, you'll do nicely, Ms. Callahan."

She pulled her hands away from him, fighting a flicker of disappointment in him for taking her consent for granted, treating her like a property, like a script in dire need of a deft touch.

"I haven't yet agreed to anything, Dr. Cameron. Least of all the undergoing of little details to transform me into the image of your wife."

"Forgive me." His features collapsed in regret. He swallowed anxiously. Distress leaked out of him like sweat. "Please. It's only that Olivia—" He broke off and began again. "Perhaps if I explain—"

"Yes." Delia straightened and shrugged out of her coat. "You've no idea the strain, Abbie, of Dr. Cameron's situation."

Abbie felt sudden regret. Delia was right. With all that had happened to his wife and the Simons family, Cameron had to be suffering a great deal. "Please. Don't give it another thought. But I'm afraid you're grasping at straws if you believe I could pull off even a mediocre impersonation of your wife."

"Perhaps." His bright eyes dulled. He studied his own freckled hands. "Perhaps. But I must ask if you would be willing to try. It's a matter of Olivia's sanity—and perhaps her life."

He led the way from the foyer into a larger room. By any standards of modern hotels, even this space was cramped and funky. He sat on the end of the double bed and indicated where Abbie should sit. Delia turned a desk chair around and recapped what she had already told Abbie, that Olivia had suffered the miscarriage, the loss of her brother, the threats to her own life and that of her father's.

Cameron nodded and sighed deeply. "Well. As to your role, Ms. Callahan. My wife is unable even to go out into public, not to mention performing her various charitable functions. Her inability only serves to reinforce her suffering. She is deeply embarrassed by this—even humiliated.''

''I don't understand. Who could possibly blame her for going into seclusion after all that has happened?'' Abbie protested.

''The point, my dear, is that Olivia blames herself. She is a Simons, the patron and sponsor of several vital and desperately needy charities. She is my wife. I am a psychiatrist, and this fact is well-known. If she is not in the public eye, if she withdraws, what does that say about the skills of her husband?''

''That you're taking care of her, protecting her when she's most vulnerable,'' Abbie offered gently. ''That can't be taken as a reflection against either of you—''

''Ah, but in Olivia's eyes . . . Think about it, Ms. Callahan. Olivia Simons Cameron is an extraordinarily wealthy woman who has invested her entire self-worth in service to her community. What kind of example does she set by caving in to adversity, however great or small? What kind of fraud must I be, if I cannot help my own wife through this desperate and dangerous time?''

He broke off, his voice cracking under the strain. From any other man, a man of less integrity, the question of his being labeled a fraud might have smacked of a terrible self-interest. Instead his failure to help his wife seemed to Abbie to slice into the heart of his own opinion of himself.

''So, you would want me to attend your wife's charity functions in her stead?'' No one, Abbie knew, did more for the cause of abused, runaway and stolen children, than Olivia Simons Cameron.

He nodded. "And the occasional social function at which we are expected."

"Do you truly believe her friends and associates would be fooled? By me?"

Cameron retrieved a portfolio from the briefcase beside the bed and handed it to her. Abbie kick off a pump and sat on her foot, then looked carefully through the photographs of Olivia Simons Cameron.

The resemblance certainly wasn't overwhelming. No one in Abbie's solidly ordinary life had ever mistaken her for Olivia, or even commented on the likeness. They shared flighty white-blond hair, but the flamboyant celebrity hairdresser Geoffrey Greystoke tended Olivia's tresses while Abbie haunted the nearest Great Clips.

She could see that they had in common certain thin, fine features. But media mavens inevitably characterized Olivia's features as "sculpted" while Abbie's Hollywood backlot studio friends held her up for the Waif Awards.

Olivia's body shape differed from Abbie's—though they were both tall and long-necked, Abbie was thin in the shoulders and bust and hips compared to Olivia's more lush proportions. This difference was what Cameron commented on.

"People see what they expect to see," Cameron said as Abbie closed the portfolio. "No one expects Olivia to be quite herself. It would be assumed that she has lost weight under the strain." He took back the portfolio. "As to standing in for her, Olivia's social secretary has agreed to assist you in every way possible. If there are lapses—little mistakes on your part, they will likewise be chalked up to the terrible toll on Olivia of our family tragedies." He paused. "I believe it would take an enormous weight from her shoulders."

Abbie felt something amiss, something vaguely disturbing at the edge of her mind. Maybe it was the way her mind worked, the way drama so often played out, the way seemingly noble motives twisted in on themselves and became sinister and self-serving. Charles Cameron was an honorable man, and he was representing his intentions as coming from only the deepest concern for Olivia. Still, Abbie had to ask the question.

"Does your wife see all this as lifting a burden from her shoulders?"

He sighed heavily. "I can't speak for her."

"If I asked her if she wants someone to take her place? To impersonate her in her public obligations?" Abbie pressed.

Cameron gave a sad smile. "Am I, in other words, coercing her into a ruse which might finally destroy her emotional well-being?"

Abbie swallowed hard but let his version of her question go unanswered.

He met her eyes steadily. "Ms. Callahan, I applaud your skepticism. I not only understand, I *approve* of your posing the question. But what is in Olivia's best interests is in mine, as well. At the moment, my wife is in such terrible pain over the miscarriage and the loss of her brother—and in the wake of her father's stroke—that she cannot begin to think clearly."

"Dr. Cameron—"

"If there is any chance at all," he insisted, "that your acting on my wife's behalf will relieve the pressure she puts on herself, then I favor it."

Abbie shook her head slowly. "I'm sorry, Dr. Cameron, but no. I don't believe a woman like your wife will appreciate your solution, or that she's likely to cut herself any slack even if you proceeded." Any more than Abbie ever did herself. "If I were Olivia, I would feel very threatened—"

"In what way?" Cameron demanded.

"Usurped—"

"No!"

"I would feel cut out of my own life," Abbie persisted, "by the mere possibility of someone taking my place." She hesitated. "Dr. Cameron, your solution feels manipulative to me. Have you thought this out carefully? Surely Olivia's friends—the people who truly love and admire her—would understand if she took a . . . a sort of leave of absence from her obligations."

"They would. Olivia would not. But all this is only a prelude to the real issue."

"Which is what?" Abbie asked.

Cameron sighed deeply and sat a moment massaging his eyes with a stubby thumb and forefinger. Finally he looked directly at Abbie. "I've brought along a videotape. If you would at least do me the courtesy of viewing it before you decide, you will understand."

Abbie inclined her head. "I can't imagine what difference—"

"Please."

"Abbie," Delia put in, "you were flown here at Dr. Cameron's expense. You may refuse his offer, but . . . the video is only eight minutes long."

A shiver passed over her flesh, but Abbie agreed to view the tape.

Cameron lost no time. Rising from the end of the bed, he closed the curtains, opened the doors of an armoire, and fed a videocassette into the VCR nested atop the television. "This is taken from the surveillance cameras on our estate. You'll see Olivia and her personal bodyguard, whom I hired through Delia to augment the estate security when the threats on her life began." He fell silent and allowed the tape to speak for itself.

A man and woman walked into the range of the camera on the descending slope of a lawn toward what Abbie assumed must be the Potomac River. The film flickered in grainy resolution. The quality of the wide-angle-lens video left a lot to be desired, but Abbie sat mesmerized, put off and provoked and fascinated by the image of herself, and not herself.

The feminine figure in leggings and a cape, captured on the videotape in the company of her bodyguard, was Olivia Simons Cameron. Something in the way she moved, or in the shape of her long legs or the animation of her gestures reminded Abbie quite eerily of herself.

Despite the countless times Olivia's photos appeared in everything from the tell-all tabloid rags to *Town & Country* riches, Abbie would never have seen the likeness to herself. It was a stretch even viewing the photos Cameron had just given her. Seeing Olivia move through the grainy, flickering surveillance video changed all that.

Cameron must have picked up on Abbie's subtle alarm. "Startling, isn't it?"

"Yes," Abbie mused. But the likeness was more than startling. It went beyond the same color of hair, deeper than the shape of her hands. Abbie couldn't know how she looked from a distance when she walked or huddled deeply into her coat as Olivia did in the surveillance video. But on some instinctive level, Abbie knew Charles Cameron was not wrong. If Olivia had a double on this earth, Abbie was probably the one.

The video flickered silently on. Olivia grew more animated, stopping, turning her back to the Potomac River to the rear of the Cameron estate, gesturing unhappily in the wind catching hold of her hair.

Abbie didn't think the wind had anything to do with Olivia's distress. Her bodyguard reached out to contain her anger but she batted his hands away, then jerked around. Though her back was toward the camera, Abbie could see that she'd brought her hands up to bury her face as if she were crying. The bodyguard cocked a hip to the side, planted a fist and shook his head, not knowing what to do with her.

Abbie slid a glance toward Charles Cameron to observe his reaction. His throat seemed locked, the tendons in his neck drawn and tight. His wife's suffering clawed at him.

Abbie's own throat thickened. Charles Cameron's powerful emotion clawed at her. She didn't consider herself an easy mark. From the hundreds of scripts she had read, she recognized a cheap pitch for quick, hot emotions, a bid for easy sympathy, when she saw it. What Abbie saw in Cameron was genuine empathy, real gut-level pain for his wife's inordinate suffering. Whatever doubts she harbored about Cameron's search for someone to act in Olivia's stead were laid to rest.

Abbie refocused on the surveillance video. A barely perceptible motion in the background of the Potomac snagged her attention and she knew by some terrible intuition that she was about to witness an attempt on Olivia's life.

In the video, her bodyguard tensed, moved warily, instinctively unnerved, attempting to protect her, to pull her away, back toward the house. She turned and jerked away from him, then stumbled and fell on the embankment, and in the next eerily silent split second, her bodyguard took what must have been a barrage of bullets in the back. His body jerked like a rag doll, and he fell forward, gushing blood, almost certainly already dead atop Olivia's prone and thrashing figure.

IN DELIA BARRY'S perfect world, Sean Baldwin wouldn't have known who preceded him on assignment as personal bodyguard to Olivia Simons Cameron, daughter of elder statesman Avery Simons and the wife of Dr. Charles Langston Cameron III.

Sean knew. Secrets were safe with him, but not from him.

Downshifting into the curve along the North Carolina coast, headed toward the funeral of Olivia Cameron's last personal bodyguard, Sean gave a mental shrug. Delia Barry would never know, or if she did, Sean didn't give a tinker's damn.

On a professional level, all his far-reaching contacts made his work a far more valuable commodity than Delia Barry could ever fully understand or appreciate. He made it his business to know the scuttlebutt, what and who was going down, and when he didn't, he knew where to go to find it.

He never lacked for company or camaraderie. He wasn't without female attentions, but he wasn't often looking, either. When he took that step beyond friendship with a woman, things got too complicated, feelings too raw for him, needs yawned too deep. So among his many friends he counted even more women than men.

He valued more than anything else the fact that he had friends everywhere, and he counted himself a friend to a great many people. Today he would see one of them buried, and the fact left a bitter taste in his mouth.

It was said there are three kinds of bodyguards. There were the thugs, the bodyguards to low-level drug dealers, protection racketeers, name your crime—akin to bouncers spoiling for a fight, for any excuse to drop the enemy.

The second kind catered to celebrity. Attracted to the lights and cameras, to the opulence and antics of their clients, the bodyguards of celebrities craved a slice of the limelight, however thin and fleeting and anonymous.

Sean had long since opted out of the circus atmosphere, which put him solidly into the third category. He'd come from the ranks of the Secret Service and he understood the delicate balance between fading into the woodwork and maintaining a presence that preempted trouble. He was arrogant and knew it, but when lives were at stake, there was no room for dithering over the politically correct and socially acceptable.

The attitude earned him an early out from the Service. The private sector protection industry had no such qualms.

He turned onto the sedate, tree-lined road leading through the gates and into the cemetery, following the map he had memorized to the grave site of his dead friend.

He parked his utilitarian bronze-colored four-wheel drive a ways down the lane and walked to the edge of the small gathering. The widow stood with her two small boys at the casket. The minister began his dust-unto-dust spiel. Sean's throat tightened. He didn't want to hear it. Didn't want to believe this had happened.

His friend's widow wept, his small boys were unnaturally still, confused and heartbroken. Sean saw himself in the older one, who was only five. Saw the terror, the uncertainty, the grim finality dawning.

Sean's father was still alive, but the year Sean turned five his father returned from Vietnam one uncelebrated miracle short of a body bag. His dad, whom he loved so fiercely it hurt, had been transformed in the space of seventeen weeks on the other side of the world into a crippled and bitter son of a bitch who was drunk or stoned or both for the next twenty years. He was a man who'd as soon beat the hell out of his kid as look at him. Sean took the beatings, then learned to duck, then began to swing back when his mom had more babies—more targets for his dad's unending anger.

So while he ached for his friend's death, he hurt more for the wife and those innocent little boys who would never get over losing their dad. It was what motivated everything Sean did, what drew him to safeguarding the lives of every client he signed on to protect.

The minister concluded his remarks. The twenty-one gun salute sundered the air in three bursts, seven rifles. The flag was taken from the casket, folded and handed to the widow with the thanks of the people and armed forces of the United States government, for the years Sean's friend had served before becoming a bodyguard in the private sector.

The widow turned, her pretty Hispanic face tear-streaked and haggard, to greet friends and family, those who had come to the grave site. The boys caught sight of Sean and broke away from their mother, running to him as if he could make this all go away.

He had only met the little boys twice before, but he understood. He remembered himself latching on to the leg of a total stranger who befriended his mom at church and only reminded him of his dad before Vietnam.

He caught them up, one in each arm, and held them close. The scent of their freshly scrubbed little bodies, the scent of innocence, picked wide open ancient, emotional scabs in Sean.

He tossed the boys around for a few minutes, earning a couple of wild shrieks of laughter-turned-back-to-tears, then handed them over to their grandparents. He held the widow close for a few moments, murmured his pathetic condolences, kissed her wet cheek, then departed.

He drove hard, north toward D.C. and his assignment to guarding the life of Olivia Cameron. Yeah, he knew a lot of people. Knowing people who knew things inevitably gave him an advantage. He would need that kind of edge because he didn't intend to be the next to die.

Chapter Two

Abbie's stomach turned and her heart thudded painfully. The attack, captured on this video, had come from the river, but the boat being used by the murderer had vanished from the surveillance video as if into thin air.

From the bottom of the screen Charles Cameron himself and two other armed guards came running across the expanse of lawn toward the river, toward Olivia. Scrambling desperately from beneath the dead, leaden weight of her bodyguard, she got up and ran screaming back toward the house. Her cape was sodden and stained with blood, her face contorted even from the impersonal distance of the surveillance video.

In her hysteria, Olivia lashed out at the men, but then Cameron was there to take charge while the estate guards covered their retreat against further attacks from the river or periphery of the estate.

In the film, Olivia fought even her husband, but he trapped her arms against her body, held her tight, cupped her head, buried his face next to her ear.

If Olivia had grown agoraphobic, terrified to leave home, afraid of benign shadows, she had good reason. Ample enough reason to warn Abbie off going anywhere near the Cameron estate herself.

Someone had it out for the extraordinarily wealthy, privileged and yet beloved Simons family.

Still, Abbie sat transfixed, her heart lodged too near her throat. The love of Charles Cameron for his wife shouted itself from the gruesome videotape, the kind of love Abbie wanted for herself, the kind of man she wanted, who would love and protect and hold her no matter what, in the worst of circumstances.

Beside her, Charles Cameron held the remote control out and punched a button with his thumb. The television screen flickered to black.

He took a deep breath and collapsed back onto the edge of the double bed. Tears had settled into the fine wrinkles beneath his eyes. "You see, Ms. Callahan, it is not the good opinion of my wife's friends but the existence of her enemies that concern me. I am not asking you simply to act in my wife's stead at her various functions. Any one of her colleagues would be more than willing to fill in for her—she is not willing to ask, as I said. But what matters, what is vital, is that whoever is out there making these obscene attempts on her life *must be stopped.*"

Abbie's lungs simply stopped. The phrase reverberated in her mind beneath the pounding of her heart in her ears. What Cameron intended was to use her to bait the madman bent on Olivia's destruction, so it was Abbie's own life at stake here. Delia cleared her throat and went on as though Abbie were still breathing, still functioning and thinking.

She held out a photo, which Abbie reflexively took. "This is Sean Baldwin, Abbie. If you agree, he is the bodyguard who will be assigned to protect you. He has never lost a client."

Cameron sat forward again and spoke in earnest, as well. "A couple of months, Ms. Callahan, is all that I ask. Time enough to give us a chance to get this cretin who killed Peter and made the attempt on Olivia's life. You will be protected, and I will offer you, say, ten thousand dollars per week? You would still be able, I think, to receive and work on whatever film scripts you choose."

His offer was wildly generous—more than generous, but Abbie stared at the face of the man they believed could manage to keep her alive while she acted as if she were Olivia.

Sean Baldwin.

He had a strong, masculine nose and full lips, a jaw to send casting directors into spasms of joy. His eyes were deep-set, his brow strong, his curling dark hair carelessly barbered. He would not stand out in a room of Chippendale models, but something about him reminded Abbie of Clark Kent, of a man who appeared ordinary, but wasn't.

Somehow, none of it mattered, not the money, not the man, not the promise of the finest protection. What mattered was that Abbie had been offered the chance to take a stand, to live up to the values her father had died for, that life was sacred and that taking it was the highest crime against humanity. That such evil must be stopped at the expense of one's own life because evil thrived where men and women of good conscience stood by, too scared to take a stand, and let it happen.

Abbie's best friend was Bibi Schorkov, a woman who'd grown up less than fifty miles from Chernobyl. Her younger brother was fighting a lymphoma she blamed on the nuclear meltdown. Bibi always mocked Abbie and her American movies for the happily-ever-after, justice-will-out, good-guys-triumph endings, but Abbie believed in them with all her heart.

In real life, things didn't always turn out as they should. The good guys didn't always win, and Bibi would be outraged that Abbie would even consider putting herself between Olivia Cameron and whoever it was who wanted her dead. But to Abbie's way of thinking, when the good guys didn't win in life it was because real people hadn't stood up to be counted for what was right and against what was wrong.

Her father had stepped into the line of fire protecting a teenage gang member. David Estevez was now a parole officer in the trenches of the Los Angeles barrio, a man committed to making a difference. Was it worth her father's life? In a heartbeat, he would have answered yes.

Some people might see Olivia as little more than a wealthy socialite, spending more on her manicures than most families spent on groceries in a week. Abbie didn't think there was any more important job in any civilization than taking care of the children. What Olivia had accomplished to that end, by founding and then endowing Child Search, put her in a league with a barrio boy like David, with Abbie's own father. She was someone who was making a difference in the world. And now she needed help.

"Would you like time to think it over?" Cameron asked.

"No." She had promised herself she would not make another blind leap of faith, but this simply didn't qualify as blind. Impersonating Olivia Cameron might get her killed.

Her mouth went dry as desert dust, but Abbie took a deep breath and plunged into harm's way. "I won't need any time, Dr. Cameron. I would be honored to fill in for your wife."

ON THE NIGHT of the Child Search Charity Masquerade Ball, the security cameras on the Cameron estate failed. Sean Baldwin was adjusting the cummerbund on his monkey-suit tux when the images on seventeen separate monitors housed in a room above the seven-car garage flickered once and then crashed altogether.

The video technician relayed the failure by a general radio dispatch to the half dozen security guards deployed around the estate. Sean listened as each one answered back in turn and was directed by the deadly calm voice of the security chief into swift, efficient action, searching the house and estate for the cause of the surveillance failure.

"Basye," the security chief commanded, "alert Cameron. Get him to his wife's suite, *now*. Baldwin, you know what to do."

Though he had spent the past week overseeing the security arrangements at the five-star D.C. hotel for the masquerade ball—by definition, a security nightmare—Sean's responsibility as bodyguard was the personal safety of Olivia Simons Cameron.

He stuffed his earpiece into place with the flesh-colored coil disappearing beneath his collar, flicked his wrist to check his own mike and then pulled his 9 mm handgun from its shoulder holster. Within fifteen seconds of the cameras going dark, he departed the surveillance room on a beeline to Olivia's suite.

Every cell in his lean, taut body attuned to possible threats, he found his way by rote memory of the blueprints of the twelve-thousand-square-foot home. Consumed with refining the security measures at the hotel, he had not met Olivia Cameron, nor had he been to her suite of rooms—but there were few more recognizable faces in the nation than hers.

He crossed paths with Basye, who'd been sent to alert Charles Cameron to the breach of security. Basye was by then checking windows and outside access doors. Neither of them said a word; neither had to say anything. It was in their body language that nothing so far had been found anywhere amiss.

As Sean arrived at the door to the suite he knew belonged to Olivia, he received instructions via the tiny receiver in his ear to send Jessica Sagermeyer, the maid attending Olivia, to the servant quarters wing for immediate questioning.

He rapped on the door, then entered without an invitation, flatly ignoring compliance with the strict unspoken code of discretion with his employers and their privacy. The thin, haughty, middle-aged Jessica was halfway to answering the door, and clearly taken aback by his unauthorized invasion of her mistress's space.

"You're history, Mr. Baldwin," she snapped. "How dare you barge in here like this!"

"Save it," he commanded. "Where is Mrs. Cameron?"

"In her dressing room if it's any—"

"It is," he interrupted grimly. Crossing the marble floor he felt himself unnerved by the modest dimensions of the room, which reminded him that he had been vaguely troubled by the blueprints. Though elegant and expensively furnished, this was clearly not the master suite, not where he would have expected to find Olivia Cameron. He mistrusted at a deep, instinctive level such unlikely arrangements as this.

He took Jessica by her upper arm and propelled her toward the door. "There's been a breach of security on the estate. Get yourself to the servant quarters and do it now. Shut the door on your way out."

She straightened, quite a feat for her already stiff, ramrod posture. Alarmed, she started to ask for details. Sean shook his head and forcibly, but more gently now, nudged her toward the door. He strode to the curtained sliding-glass door leading onto a sun room, at the edge of his mind registering the maid's departure along with every detail of the sitting room, then checked the expansive wall of glass for intruders or breaches from one end to the other.

Satisfied that there were none, and that in the windowless dressing room Olivia Cameron was safe, he repeated the procedure in the sun room itself. Listening to the radio in his ear as the estate guards began to report no intruders found, he reentered the bedroom.

He closed and locked the sliding-glass door behind him, rearmed the alarms, then focused his senses on the movements of Olivia Simons Cameron in the adjoining room. He first heard her humming softly, and knew she must still be oblivious to his presence and the threat of estate cameras gone dark.

The door to the bathroom, which also led to the dressing room, stood only slightly ajar, but he could see in the wall-mounted mirror a six-by-six skylight. He was advised, then, that the cause of the video failure had been found—an electrical breaker had somehow tripped itself, cutting off power to the estate security cameras.

Something more to add to the unlikely.

He would not leave off without assuring himself of Olivia's safety. He needed to check that the skylight over her most private rooms had not been tampered with. He shoved open the dressing room door.

When he did, what he saw in the mirror was his client, the wife of his employer, pulling the bodice of an antique gown into place over her bare, exquisite breasts. His body reacted swiftly, heatedly, and because of it, Sean took a fierce and instant dislike to the lovely Olivia Simons Cameron.

ABBIE'S KNEES LOCKED. None of her week-long stint of training in the art of being Olivia Simons Cameron had prepared her for this flagrant intrusion. Or for the wild thump of her heart, or the glint of the real live gun he held, or the smothering heat spreading upward from her navel to her nape. Though they had not met, she recognized Sean Baldwin from his pictures.

His intrusion must mean she was somehow in danger, at risk. Clutching the bodice of her gown, she shivered violently. "What's wrong?"

His clean-shaven jaw tightened, his eyes narrowed. He peeled his eyes off her and refocused up at the skylight, then turned his blue-black eyes back on her.

Finally he answered her. "There's been a breakdown in the surveillance equipment."

Abbie blanched. "What does that mean, a breakdown? Are you saying . . . is there an intruder?"

"Apparently not." He reached inside his coat jacket and holstered the gun beneath his left armpit.

"Then you're here because . . ."

"Estate security has only just called an 'all clear.'"

She nodded jerkily, folding her arms over the part of her bare chest the dress didn't cover. "You're certain?"

He lifted one shoulder in a shrug. The tuxedo jacket moved exquisitely with his upper body. "The only thing I'm personally certain of," he answered, "is that no windows or doors have been tampered with here in...your quarters."

His voice played on her nerves more than the possibility of an intruder had, lilting with the deep, masculine sounds of a second or third generation Scotsman. He managed in that single sentence to convey suspicion of her, or her "quarters," and of the so-called "all clear."

He suspected these were not Olivia's quarters, every bit as much as he disliked writing off even a fleeting breakdown in surveillance to coincidence.

Abbie swallowed hard, suddenly aware that his suspicions sharpened his instincts, made him into what he was, made him the bodyguard who'd never lost a client, but he scared her, threatened her at some level she didn't even understand.

"Where is Jessica?"

"Where's your husband?" he countered. "Cameron should have been at your side even before I got here."

"No, he shouldn't. He—" She broke off short of saying he should be with his wife. She'd made a mistake to feed Sean Baldwin's suspicions, which he may let lie, but would not forget.

He wasn't supposed to know she wasn't Olivia. Did he know anyway? "I'm sure Charles will be here any minute." Summoning all the command Olivia might have shown, Abbie turned away from Baldwin.

She couldn't avoid his image in the mirror. He leaned into the doorjamb and folded his arms over his chest. He was a big man, much bigger than Abbie had supposed. Six-five, at least, in a black tuxedo that had to have been tailor-made to so easily accommodate his broad shoulders... and holster.

She dragged her gaze off his mirror image and wrapped her arms around her midriff to hold the undone mauve satin bodice in place. "Please go now... and send Jessica back."

"She's being questioned in the servant quarters."

"Why?"

"SOP—standard operating procedure. Every member of the household will be questioned when a security breach like this happens."

"If the danger has passed, I need her," Abbie retorted. "Unless you would like to handle the thirty-five buttons down the back of my gown?"

He blinked slowly. "I don't like games, Mrs. Cameron."

Abbie shrugged. His eyes never left her, his attention never wandered. The heated flush clung to her. He unnerved her on every level. She reacted out of pure pretense to the aplomb she supposed Olivia possessed in better times.

"The buttons need doing up, Mr. Baldwin. If I were in any real danger, matters might be different, but if you're right, I'm not. I must be at the hotel at least an hour before the ball. I'll be late if we don't leave in the next few minutes."

His arms were crossed over his chest. He barely had to move to speak into the microphone at his wrist.

"Send Mrs. Cameron's maid back to her suite." Still, his eyes never left Abbie. "You'll need her," he said, "to get back into street clothes and pack your ball-gown."

For a moment Abbie could only stare at him. "Are you mad? Have you any idea how many petticoats, how—" She broke off again. The intricacies of her undergarments were nothing she wanted to explain to him. She wanted to slap the half-cocky, all-masculine smirk from his face. "I see no point in changing arrangements that were in place days ago—"

"Which is exactly my point," he interrupted.

"Or any sense," she insisted, "in dressing again at the hotel when I'm only—"

"Thirty-five buttons short of being dressed already?" One black, stalwart eyebrow raised. "Let me try—once—to make sense of it for you, Mrs. Cameron.

"Your last bodyguard got himself shot to smithereens in your stead. Remember? Remember him jerking while the bullets slammed into him? Do you remember the look in his eyes, Mrs. Cameron? Do you remember the smell of blood and fear pouring out of him, right there on top of you, right here on your exorbitantly protected estate?"

Abbie flashed on the videotape she'd seen in Charles Cameron's hotel room. It had made her feel sick, but not so sick as if she had been there, doing that, feeling the dead weight of a man bleeding out his life, drawing his last ragged breath at her breast. Baldwin's pitiless sketch of what Olivia had gone through in that shattering instant made Abbie feel hollow and sick and scared inside, and she couldn't break off meeting the dark, angry eyes of the dead bodyguard's replacement.

"You'll forgive me," Baldwin warned softly, "if I don't give a *damn* how many petticoats you have to peel out of. Or the number of buttons you have to fuss with."

Finally she was able to look away. For her own safety, she would have to do as she was told. "How soon do we leave?"

"As soon as you no longer look as if you've even heard of the masquerade ball. Ten minutes."

She tilted her chin up, desperate to reassert some control, somewhere. "Then perhaps you'll see to bringing the limousine around."

He blinked and shook his head as if he couldn't believe her nerve or cheekiness. "Did you think you'd just take me down a few notches on the food chain?"

She stood there stiffly, willing herself to breathe, fighting to maintain her composure.

"I'd be amused, Mrs. Cameron, except that tonight I am not only in charge of your every move, I *am* the chauffeur. The limousine is taking a spin or two around the Beltway and returning here. A decoy, if you will. The security team in costume for the ball will travel to the hotel with your husband in his Mercedes." He straightened from leaning into the doorjamb and turned to leave, then looked back for a brief moment.

"You and I..." His dark eyes narrowed. Considering that she should have felt safe in his presence, she had never felt more insecure, more exposed. *You and I...* For a split second the atmosphere between them smelled of ozone to her, as if lightning had struck and the oxygen sizzled to its most unstable form, and then it was over.

Phantom lightning, here and gone quicker than she could breathe or blink.

"You and I," he said, like talking to a log now, "will be taking my four-wheel drive. Try to remember what's at stake, Mrs. Cameron. Someone out there wants you dead."

IT WASN'T OUT of some defiant misguided attempt at reasserting control that Abbie was late in meeting Baldwin's ten-minute ultimatum. Not even packing the antique gown with its hoop skirt and layers of petticoats into a suitcase meant to draw no special attention would take all that long.

But after Sean Baldwin left her to dress down, Abbie got the shakes so bad she couldn't even hook her bra or find both armholes of her U.C. Irvine sweatshirt. She could almost find a way to put aside what had gone on between them, but not the reminder.

Someone out there wants you dead.

She'd been clueless, before. *This* was the fear Olivia couldn't deal with, and Abbie had blithely agreed to do it for her without understanding the least thing about what facing your own death really meant.

When Jessica knocked, Abbie sent her away. The last thing she needed was to come unglued in front of Olivia's maid—and she was coming undone. To keep moving, she whispered to herself, over and over again, *He'll keep you alive, he'll keep you alive,* but she didn't know if she could count on it. Or if the only thing she could count on was that he would be next, falling on top of her, bleeding out, dying.

She slipped off all the petticoats at once and pulled on a pair of her own jeans over the garter belt and sheer silk stockings. She broke her thumbnail to its quick just trying to get her jeans zipped.

Picking at her broken thumbnail through wavering, angry tears, she knew absolutely that she wasn't cut out for this. She should be back home in California, carrying in dinner to her landlord whose lover was dying of AIDS complications, or working her way through a pile of scripts or going to her *astanga* yoga class, or baby-sitting for the reed-thin studio receptionist who was too young to handle a normal, healthy baby, let alone the one she got, a tiny little girl born with spina bifida.

That was the kind of stuff Abbie handled every day. This was not. She knew without a single doubt that she should be woman enough to just stand up and say this wasn't her forte.

She'd do that. She'd march out in her jeans and sweatshirt and admit that she couldn't pull off this impersonation of one of the country's most-watched socialites.

She rasped away with a nail file at what was left of her own nail beneath the broken phony one. She'd arrived on the Cameron estate only four and a half days ago. A day went into getting her hair cut in Olivia's style, the cursed acrylic nails, and a fitting for the Scarlett O'Hara ballgown to be worn at the charity ball.

She'd spent hours on end with Enid Schomp, Olivia's social secretary, in grueling run-throughs of names and photos, pastimes and foibles of Olivia's closest friends and associates.

Then Charles Cameron himself started in on her, coaching Abbie in his wife's mannerisms, her style of speaking, her humor, her grace, the tilt of her head, her smile, her moue, her . . . the list went endlessly on.

Most of Abbie's indoctrination went on in Olivia's presence. They had first met within an hour of Abbie's arrival on the estate.

The woman's suite glowed richly in navy and peach tones. The floor was marble, the carpet, a hugely expensive Karastan original, the furniture lacquered and polished to a high, unblemished sheen. Everything down to the understated paisley silk damask-covered goosedown comforter on the custom bed half again as large as a king-size reflected the discriminating taste of the woman who lived here.

Her dressing table was lighted by fixtures carved from a rare Italian marble. The bath was sunk into a raised pedestal and matched the size of a five-person hot tub. A kitchen as large as Abbie's own was equipped with an espresso machine, a microwave, refrigerator, water purifier and three-burner stovetop.

Most people lived in less square footage than Olivia's master bedroom occupied. Cameron seemed not to fit. Familiar, yes, but comfortable? Abbie didn't think so, but she chalked it up to the eggshells he seemed to walk on with his jumpy, fragile, beloved Olivia.

Sachi, on the other hand, ruled. The basset hound was a beautiful dog, but her constant whining wore on everyone's nerves. Everyone but Olivia. Without her dog, Olivia would have been in even worse emotional straits.

Olivia had not left her suite since the day her bodyguard was murdered in her stead. Instead, she'd flatly refused to move out of them when Abbie came, even in the interest of safeguarding her life against an attacker who might know exactly which rooms inside the house belonged to her.

When Abbie first saw her, Olivia Simons Cameron was standing in the lanai off her bedroom beyond a closed set of elegant white-lacquered French doors. Beyond the designer hothouse windows, Abbie could see backhoes tearing up the lawn at the far end of the estate, close to the river.

She'd asked Cameron about it. "What's going on?"

Overcome with emotion, he shook his head. "She's terrified, Abbie. She needs walls. She needs to know what happened down there—" He gulped, stopped. Cleared his throat. "That what happened down there won't ever happen again."

He'd ordered fifteen-foot stone walls built at the perimeter of the estate, five feet beyond the original wrought iron. The incredible view to the river would be lost, but Charles Cameron would put up the fence and then he would pay to take it down again if it bought Olivia the peace of mind she so desperately needed.

He'd opened the French doors onto the lanai, which was filled with exotic plants, perfectly controlled heat and humidity. Olivia turned at the interruption. The moment she laid eyes on Abbie, hostility radiated from every delicate pore.

Her hair was a mess, unkempt, pulled back in a careless ponytail. She had lost weight and looked gaunt, but Abbie was unnerved again how much alike they looked. It was as if she were looking into a carnival mirror and seeing a version of herself if her soul had simply shriveled. Olivia had turned her dulled gray-green eyes, ravaged by dark shadows, on her husband. "This is to be my replacement, Charles?"

He'd swallowed, hard. Pain glittered in his eyes. "No one can replace you, Liv. Abbie is here to learn to act in your stead until the threats against you have ended."

Olivia had refused to get up or look at either one of them. Abbie wanted to reassure Olivia that what her husband said was true, but Charles Cameron had warned her against trying. Olivia either ignored the work to transform Abbie into her clone, or endured it. Sachi whined.

Abbie had only one private conversation with Olivia in those four days, and she wished now that she'd just skipped the effort.

She had agreed, at least in part, to fill in for Olivia for the sake of what appeared to be a love affair too rare and precious between Charles Cameron and his wife. But after the attempt on Olivia's life, which was only the latest in a string of terrible personal losses, Olivia trusted no one, not her secretary, not Jessica, not Abbie, and least of all her own husband.

Four days later Abbie felt picked over, propped up, hopelessly inept at her attempts to be Olivia. Ninety-six hours of training was never going to be enough. Cameron had assured Abbie this was not the case, that she was going to pull off the impersonation quite brilliantly.

Only now, thanks to Baldwin's brutally graphic recounting of the last bodyguard's death and his parting shot, Abbie understood Olivia's fear at her own core.

She threw down the nail file and slung open one of her own suitcases on the exquisite antique Amish quilt covering the bed. *Just clam up, Abbie. He'll keep you alive. Just shut up and do this.*

She'd promised, given her word. A person carries through with what they've promised to do. She could hear her father saying it, hear his solemn tone of voice when she was only eight while he explained why she had to hand over to its rightful owners a lost dachshund puppy. She'd promised her daddy she would if the puppy's owners came looking after an ad in the lost and found.

She just hadn't thought anyone would come. Twenty years later, she just hadn't thought anyone would really threaten *her* life.

Another leap of faith.

Chapter Three

Another foolhardy decision.

She had to get a grip, had to buck up and go on. A professional should be doing this, but the reason for Abbie's decision to take Charles Cameron's offer still held true. Evil would keep marching on if people didn't stand up, one by one, against it. No one, she swore fiercely to herself, no one would ever see how scared she was.

By the time she got herself together twenty-five minutes had passed, a driving rain had begun and Baldwin was banging on her door.

She opened it with her jean jacket on and her suitcase in hand. He spared an approving glance at clothes nobody would take for anything Olivia Cameron would ever wear and then took the suitcase from her grasp.

They saw no one, not even Charles Cameron, on the way to the estate garage. She had the distinct impression Baldwin had arranged things that way, and that whatever Cameron thought of the change in plans, he'd acquiesced.

Baldwin had pulled his vehicle into the garage so she could get in without getting drenched by the rain. The bone-chilling humidity was already enough to ruin her hair. He opened the passenger door of a rugged-looking, bronze-colored four-wheel drive, then tossed her suitcase in the open rear window, closed it, got into the driver's seat—set back as far as it would go—and took off.

He stayed to the most heavily traveled roads, changing lanes often, constantly checking his mirrors out the rain-drenched windows. Abbie stayed quiet, trying to insulate herself for a little while, to go over in her mind everything she'd learned, everyone she would know if she were Olivia, and the speech she was expected to give from memory on behalf of Child Search.

After a while Baldwin began talking softly, filling her in on his expectations, on how she should behave, what she should do so she wouldn't screw up and get herself killed despite his best efforts.

"The one thing you have to remember is that if I tell you to do something, you do it. You don't think about, argue over, or ignore it, you just do it. Clear?"

"Yes." She hadn't gotten carsick in a very long time, but she could sometimes feel the start of the tires hydroplaning, and her stomach turned every time.

"Specifically," he went on, "don't ever get out of my immediate reach. If you need to use the facilities, I will take you upstairs to the private suite reserved in my name where you'll change for the ball. Your interview for the media will be done as you're arriving at the grand ballroom from upstairs."

Olivia had wanted to make an entrance on behalf of Child Search with friends and associates from outside the hotel. "Um...I—there are a lot of people who've paid a great deal of money to be seen coming in with me—"

"Everything is restaged."

"It's important."

"I know." He nodded, then cast her a quick apologetic glance. "It can't be helped. There won't be any deviations."

He whipped into the faster lane without using his blinker. The unexpected sideways motion made her sick to her stomach again. Keeping watch in both the side and rearview mirrors, he never so much as looked at her again, but he knew. "If you're feeling sick, you should put your head down between your knees."

"I'm fine."

"Yeah."

"I will be *fine*."

He shot her a look. He didn't believe her. He squinted against the bright lights of oncoming traffic at a curve in the highway and went on with his instructions. "If you need a drink, I will pour it. I'll send for food if you're hungry. It won't come from the catering kitchen. Nothing goes past your lips that I haven't provided. Still clear?"

She couldn't imagine, with the faintly nauseated taste of the motion sickness in her mouth, wanting anything. Asking him for anything. But Baldwin's list of precautions slapped her hard again with the cold hard fact that she was not conducting some innocent masquerade on Olivia Cameron's behalf, but a deadly game of cat and mouse against whoever it was who wanted her dead.

Baldwin looked hard at her, waiting for her to acknowledge his instructions. She jerked her gaze away and stared out her window, then nodded that she understood.

"All right." He downshifted behind a slow-moving van. "Lastly, then, if you choose to dance with anyone other than your husband—or me—your partner will first be gone over with a metal detector wand."

It wasn't enough, Abbie thought, that as recently as two hours ago she'd believed it would take all her concentration just to pull off a decent impersonation of Olivia. Now she had all these caveats, and more, like what he meant about dancing with him, to deal with.

"Isn't it a bit beyond the pale, to expect O—our friends to be searched like that?"

"No." He shook his head, and glanced at her. "None of this is negotiable."

"Fine." She jerked her head to the side, agreeing without giving him the benefit of staring her down. But she couldn't keep quiet. "I thought it was unlikely that an attempt would be made on my life—"

"That would depend on whether the murderer is the sort to get off on killing you with all your friends looking on."

She plowed on. "But in...in such a crowded setting. Surely there are too many people, too many witnesses—"

"A crowd becomes a mob in under five seconds," he interrupted again. His tone made it imminently clear he didn't care who had agreed with whom on whether or not a charity ball was a likely occasion for her murder. "In a mob, a killer has the advantage—he gets swallowed up and disappears forever." His brow creased. "Do you really believe you know who you can trust?"

A bubble of laughter escaped her.

He gave her a look. She felt that disorienting sensation again, of an illicit sexual attraction between them conflicting with his active dislike of her.

"A touch of hysteria, Mrs. Cameron?" he asked softly.

"Olivia," she corrected, sick of his calling her Mrs. Cameron.

"Fine. You want a first-name basis, you've got it. Sean."

"Sean," she agreed. "You could call it that." Since she didn't know anyone at all, not to mention whom she could trust among Olivia and Charles's friends, a touch of hysteria was a conservative reaction. "Considering my life is in such danger, I don't think it's so unusual."

He said nothing. She wanted to goad him into saying to her face that he didn't like her. She wanted him to explain that. She wanted to know what the sexual buzz between them was about if he disliked her so much—but of course, she couldn't. She was supposed to be Charles Cameron's wife, and Sean Baldwin had already called her on playing games.

In her heart, Abbie was a secret keeper. She didn't blurt out her own feelings, not to anyone. Her friends complained all the time that getting so much as the weather forecast out of her required a crowbar. Especially Bibi, who'd grown up in the Ukraine and had learned to keep her mouth shut from the time she'd learned to talk. Even by Bibi's standards, Abbie was secretive with what she knew and felt and shared with anyone.

But Abbie dearly wanted to tell Sean Baldwin she wasn't Olivia.

She wanted to confide the truth because keeping up more than one charade at a time was like juggling one too many hand grenades. One of them was bound to slip her grasp and explode at her feet. She had already slipped twice, and she knew he'd noticed.

But there was more. She wanted to know which was real, the attraction between them or his obvious dislike of her, or both, and whether or not—even if he didn't like her version of Olivia Cameron—he would like Abbie Callahan, and pursue the attraction, if he learned she wasn't Olivia.

But that was all material for a romantic comedy with a Sandra Bullock heroine and a Schwarzenegger hero. She couldn't tell Sean Baldwin anything. Cameron had been insistent on the point—her bodyguard must believe he was protecting the real Olivia.

Between pulling off her impersonation and staying alive, Abbie had more than enough to think about. The last thing she needed was to give in to some perverse attraction to her bodyguard—a man who already disliked her, and believed she was someone else's wife.

At the hotel, he took her in through the kitchen and up the service elevator. They were met at the door of the rooms he had reserved in his name by the hotel manager and a maid designated to help Abbie get back into the Scarlett O'Hara ballgown.

When she emerged from the dressing room, she found Charles Cameron storming in the door, reminding Sean Baldwin who it was paying his salary. "I don't give a damn how you rearrange the security measures, Baldwin, so long as you don't expect me to arrive separately from my wife. Another stunt like this one—"

Sean looked like he was just waiting for an ultimatum. She wanted to knock their heads together for acting like ten-year-olds.

"Charles, it's all right," Abbie interrupted softly. "You hired Mr. Baldwin to protect my life." She met his eyes again. "However boorish and...arrogant—" however much he had disliked her on sight and for reasons she couldn't begin to fathom "—he is taking seriously his responsibilities to my safety."

"Of course he is," Charles relented. "I simply want to know at every moment that you're all right." He reached for her hands. "Will you manage, Liv?"

"I'll be fine, Charles." *Bravado, Abbie,* she thought, but better that than the alternative. She could only reassure herself nothing was likely to happen, and that if it did, Sean Baldwin would handle it.

Charles squeezed her fingers. "That's my girl."

SEAN HAD SUSPECTED from the moment the surveillance equipment went dark on the Cameron estate that nothing was as it should have been. That there was a flaw somewhere not attributable at all to the equipment itself or a breaker flipping itself off. He responded by changing the rules, the arrangements, by taking Olivia Cameron himself, by taking her into the hotel by a kitchen delivery entrance, but he couldn't shake the feeling that he was missing something.

He had called the estate on his cellular while she changed back into her gown with the help of a maid on staff at the hotel. He suggested to Cameron's security chief that every checkpoint on the estate be revisited. He was assured there were no intruders, or anyone lurking nearby. Still, Sean felt that the charity ball was an elaborate cover-up for something far more sinister going down. He didn't like Charles Cameron's possessive streak, either, but he had less than nothing to say about that.

The only thing he could do was stick like a bad penny all night to the woman he had been hired to protect. He choreographed the press conference and photo ops so most of the Cameron friends and associates never noticed that Olivia was under guard.

He paced the perimeter of the dance floor, never more than three or four feet from her. True to his word, he handled her food and drink requests that, to her credit, were simple. Bottled sparkling water, a Pinot Noir, crackers. A masquerade ball was a nearly flawless opportunity for a deadly attack and she could have made his job a living nightmare.

She didn't. He wished she would so he'd have some excuse, any excuse, for disliking her on sight. He had none. He mistrusted her on some instinctive level for reasons he hadn't yet defined, but she probably didn't deserve the antagonism he was dishing out.

Like hell, Baldwin, he thought. No one survived long in his profession by ignoring instinct. No one. If he mistrusted her there was a reason. He told himself it had nothing to do with his baser instincts or his heated, overpowering reaction to her in her dressing room while she covered her breasts in purple satin.

The ballroom of the grand old hotel had grown swelteringly hot. The band took a small break and a string quartet filled in with background music. Six hundred and seventeen bodies, including the catering staff, milled about the room. The ball overhead cast prisms of light by the thousands. The pitch of conversations grew steadily, the laughter more raucous.

Sean stood behind Charles and Olivia Cameron as she conducted a receiving line to thank the Child Search donors of five thousand dollars and up. A fine sheen of perspiration clung to her bare shoulders. The heat intensified the subtle scent of her perfume.

Sean rolled his head from side to side and stuck his fingers inside his high collar in a futile attempt at cooling down and focused on each approaching guest. Amazingly it was Charles Cameron feeding his wife the names of contributors and the amounts they'd donated to Child Search.

Why?

Olivia Cameron had an executive assistant Sean would have thought a lot more likely to be the one helping her with the names, to thank the donors personally. But Cameron was looking out for his wife, and Sean appreciated the fact. Cameron had been at least as close to her at all times, all night, as Sean had been himself—with the single exception of her trip back to the sleeping suite to freshen up.

His eyes constantly roving, anticipating, Sean checked his watch and rolled his shoulders. The truth was he'd never worked for a client so compliant and willing to meet his demands as Charles Cameron. If he was for real, Sean would owe him a mental apology.

The receiving line worked its way to the end of the five thousand dollar donors with a Marie Antoinette drag queen and his date Napoleon, followed by Superman and Lois, then Hamlet, Hester Prynne, Charlie Chaplin, and finally Joan of Arc. Cameron reminded her that they'd last been with Hamlet and Hester—then Jim and Francine Quimby—on a Fourth of July weekend trip aboard the Quimby yacht.

When the donors of two to five thousand dollars began, Count Dracula presented himself. Cameron wasn't able to supply cogent details of a friendship and clearly didn't know this Dracula personally, but the Count addressed his wife as "Liv." He made a heavily accented Transylvanian parody of wanting to drink her blood, but when he put his mitts on her shoulders and bent to bite at *Liv's* beautiful long neck, Cameron bristled, she stiffened, and reflexively, Sean stepped closer.

His motion caught Count Dracula's attention; the charity donor looked up to be confronted with Sean's warning glance.

The jerk must have felt threatened and took exception. He still had hold of her shoulders, now from arm's length. His voice raised. "What the hell?"

"Move along," Sean warned quietly.

"Say what?"

"I said, get your hands off Mrs. Cameron and move along." The guy was about two-tenths of a second from a dislocated shoulder.

"Why, you..." Dracula swallowed and backed off. His Transylvanian accent had reverted to thick Southern contempt. "Liv, what's going on here? Who is this goon?"

"Um . . . Harold." She cast Sean a quelling glance. "Pay him no attention. He's just being a little over-zealous looking out for me."

Dracula fumed. "Well . . ."

One tenth of a second now, Sean thought.

"I *do* take offense, Liv. Serious offense to being treated like some kind of pond scum—"

"Don't now," Abbie interrupted in the flirty voice Cameron had drilled her in using. No man ever left

Olivia's presence, he'd told her, without feeling like she'd just coronated him. "I want to thank you personally for your contribution to Child Search. You know, there is just no one who's been a more constant pillar of the charity than you have been."

Her charm defused Dracula's anger, and he wound up whining in his obnoxious drawl. "I know you know that, Liv—"

"But it's unimportant in the bigger picture of our charity, isn't it?" She took both his hands. "You stay in touch, now, will you? Your support is so important. I'd love to hear from you soon."

Flattered and finally appeased, Dracula moved on. The costumed donors in line seemed to breathe a sigh of relief and Cameron eyed his wife with admiration.

"Well done, Liv. Well done."

But Sean knew then and there, while Cameron turned to shake his hand and thank him for rising to what amounted to nothing more than the innocuous threat of an oily but harmless Dracula, that he didn't like the patronizing tone of his employer's voice.

SEAN WAITED until the reception line, which wound up with the thousand dollar donors, had concluded. The dance band replaced the string quartet and Charles Cameron turned to his wife and began to lead her to the dance floor before Sean cut him off.

"Excuse me, sir, but I need a few minutes with your wife."

The compliant doctor hesitated, started to protest, then apparently thought better of it and graciously stepped aside.

"Of course. Liv," he said, touching her shoulder in an encouraging, possessive manner, "you'll be okay?"

She doubted it very much. The flat glint in Sean Baldwin's eyes didn't bode well for her, but Cameron had already more or less conceded. She straightened and smiled. "I'll be fine."

Cameron nodded and stroked her cheek briefly in a habitual gesture with the back of his forefinger, then turned away. Sean nodded at one of the other security men, Abbie assumed in some kind of spook-speak to cover his back while he danced with her, then pulled her into his arms.

He let a few measures go by, settling her into his rhythm, never really looking at her. "Tell me about Count Dracula," he ordered.

"Dracula." It took a stern reminder to herself that even if the Dracula character had been an empty threat, a meaningless encounter, the real threat could easily still be lurking about. Maybe Baldwin was making idle conversation, but she doubted that, too. If he was asking, he probably had a reason.

She spouted off what she remembered from her drills with Enid Schomp. "I . . . his name is Harold Lawrencian. He lives in Chevy Chase. He's an optometrist and he's been contributing to Child Search from its inception."

Sean nodded. Still studiously avoiding looking at her, he pulled her a little closer. "A loyal donor, then."

"Yes."

"Someone you know well."

Abbie hesitated. Where was he going with this? "Fairly well."

"Someone you and Dr. Cameron socialize with?"

She was on her own now, forced to improvise. She'd already told him everything she knew. She shrugged. "Occasionally."

He looked at her then. "What color are his eyes?"

"What?"

"What color," he repeated, "are Harold Lowry's eyes?"

"Lawrencian," she snapped, correcting him, irritated with him. Angry with herself for wondering how Sean went from looking at her as if he'd like to toss her on the nearest bed one moment to this cold, clinical, overbearing, obnoxious commandant-turned-inquisitor the next. "What does the color of Harold Lawrencian's eyes have to do with anything?"

"Not a thing," he granted. "Where is his office?"

"I don't remember."

"Is he *your* optometrist?"

"No."

"Who is?"

"Williams. Edward C. Williams. Check it out." Another fortunate piece of Enid's lessons, clicked into place.

"Trust me, I will."

"Good. Now if you don't mind, I'd like to get a refreshment." She started to break away, but he let her get only far enough to spin her in a dance step back to his arms.

"One more thing, Mrs. Cameron." She sighed. He scowled. "Smile," he said. "We don't want your guests to think you're not having fun."

"I'm not." She focused on his black satin tie, trying to distract herself from the heat radiating off his powerful body clashing with the chill in his voice. The flesh on her arms broke out in goose bumps. She cleared her throat. "What is it you want to know?"

"I want to know why Dr. Cameron found it necessary to remind you that you spent the Fourth of July weekend on a yacht with some of your closest friends.''

Abbie blanched, and her head spun, and he knew as well as she that if he hadn't been quick enough to catch her she would have tripped on the hoop of her own skirt. "I'm sorry," she managed, "but it's almost time for my speech. I have to go backstage now."

She broke away this time, or he let her go. She turned and began to make her way toward the exit leading to the stage. He followed her. He had to follow, but she wished he was anywhere else on the planet and it was someone else but him shadowing her every move, questioning every damned tiny detail.

She had the wild idea that he'd studied the same lists she had, the names of every person at all closely associated with Charles and Olivia Cameron. Did he know she was only parroting what she had learned?

Probably. The lists hadn't included anyone's physical description, so if she'd ever actually spent more than thirty seconds with Harold Lawrencian, she would have known what color his eyes were. The detail was only telling since she didn't know.

Everyone else present tonight saw Abbie as Olivia because Olivia was who they expected to see. Charles Cameron had been right. Knowing the emotional trauma Olivia had been through in the past several months, none of her friends would dream of challenging Abbie.

Sean Baldwin, though, hung out in a class all his own, rattling her cage because he couldn't protect her from lies and half-truths that kept cropping up. He had no prior expectations of Olivia. He obviously trusted his instincts ahead of anything else, and he wasn't going to politely back off the hard questions.

On this, Cameron had been wrong. Keeping Sean in the dark as to Abbie's being only a double to Olivia Cameron was playing him for a fool, and he wasn't having it.

She smiled and waved to a group standing nearby who called out to her, then pulled open the door herself from the ballroom onto the stairs leading up to the stage. She made it up a few of the stairs before Sean came through the door behind her.

Feeling trapped and foolish and caught up in a naughty game, another one of those half hysterical bubbles of laughter escaped her before she could get to the stage door.

"Stop." He stood at the bottom step and ordered her in a low, terse voice not to move, to stay exactly where she was.

She ignored him. He'd be even angrier, she knew, because the one thing he'd told her was crucial was that she obey him on the spot.

Too bad. Shoving through the stage door, she fled to the podium behind the curtain. On the other side of it the band musicians segued into the theme song of the Child Search organization, a piece of music that had been written at Olivia's request and donated to the cause.

Behind her she heard Sean uttering orders into his mike to the rest of the team. The backstage area had not been cleared. She knew with a grain of sense she would have recognized how foolish it was to plunge onto the backstage before security had made one last sweep of it, but in a few desperately short moments, the music would fade and the curtain would rise, and she would have to deliver Olivia's speech.

But now, the stage lights muted by the curtain cast her profile in shadow against the backdrop and she could only stand there watching Sean Baldwin's much larger shadow coming toward her.

"If you ever pull a stunt like this again, Mrs. Cameron—"

"Don't. Stop—" Stop what, Abbie? she thought. *Tell him to stop calling you Mrs. Cameron? Tell him to leave you alone and unprotected?* Olivia's murderer may have been lurking back here just waiting for a stupid, foolish mistake on her part.

There were hundreds of people waiting out there to hear Olivia's official thank you to the Child Search donors, and any one of them could be the one who wanted her dead, but she'd screwed up and let herself panic over Baldwin and his relentless questions. "Just...don't...talk to me."

"Do you understand what a stupid risk you took just now?"

"Perfectly." She couldn't take her eyes off the specter of his shadow approaching hers. The angle, the direction of the stage lights made his shadow seem closer to her than he was, and the intimacy stunned her. Despite the band, she could hear her own heart thumping.

Fear sent a wrenching spasm through her. "Please..."

His angry expression eased. He cupped her cheek with his hand. His touch was calming and wildly scary and a part of her wanted to step into his arms. He moved even closer, as if he knew that part of her. "Listen to me. If you're in trouble, I need to know it. How. Why. What's going on."

She knew he still wanted an answer, a reasonable explanation of why Olivia Cameron had to be reminded who her friends were and what she'd done with them. "I don't... always remember things. I've been under a great deal of stress. Sometimes I blank out things, names. I just didn't want that to happen tonight to the Child Search benefactors."

She pulled out every stop she could find in herself and met his dark, intense eyes straight-on. "It's very important, you know, for people to be recognized for their contributions. Child Search wouldn't exist without them."

"I don't get it. Are you asking me to believe your husband was only making sure you didn't draw a blank over the names of lifelong friends?"

"No." Abbie swallowed. The band was drawing near the final measures of the Child Search theme song. The lighting changed; their shadows on the backdrop disappeared. "No. It doesn't matter to me what you believe. All I want is for you to back off and—"

"You know I can't do that."

"Let me get this over with. And if you have any more questions, take them up with my husband."

She turned from him then and took her place behind the clear, high-tech, bulletproof podium ordered specially for this occasion. A moment later she heard Olivia's name and accomplishments over the public address system, and a moment after that, the curtains rose.

The spotlight hit her. Blinded by the light, she was greeted with a thunderous standing ovation meant for Olivia Cameron.

She bowed her head and clasped her hands and practiced breathing in the *ujjayi* manner her yoga instructors taught. She needed desperately to bring herself back to her own center, to regain her strength and equilibrium, and it wouldn't come from anywhere outside her.

Sean stood watching her from the curtains, no more than three feet away, and there wasn't a moment, despite her focused breathing, that Abbie wasn't more aware of his being there than of the obligation in front of her.

She had a job to do, people to thank on Olivia's behalf, important work to recognize on the very real issues of lost, stolen and runaway children.

Her breathing finally stiffened her resolve.

Baldwin could take his doubts and questions and stuff them all. His job was to protect her no matter who she was. Hers was to represent Olivia.

She looked at him briefly, then plunged into Olivia's speech. The more she talked, the more ardent she became. She refused to be cowed by her failure to persuade Sean Baldwin that she was who she stood there pretending to be.

Sooner or later he would know she was only a stand-in. Then, maybe, he'd bloody well realize that in spite of everything, the threats, the mistakes, his own intimidation tactics and the constant reminders that her life was on the line, she'd delivered a nearly flawless performance tonight.

And another thing, too—he wouldn't be likely to miss . . . Abbie Callahan was no pushover.

Chapter Four

The woman, Sean thought, was either the least accomplished liar or the most emotionally brittle creature he had ever known. At times he wondered if she knew her own name. At others, he knew she understood exactly the nature of the threats against her.

Whichever it was, maybe both, maybe she was schizo, she was Trouble with a capital T. Reckless, in-your-face disregard for her own safety he could handle. She became dangerous when she couldn't remember simple details of her life—like which people in a crowd were lifelong friends and which were not.

Like remembering which door led from the garage to the main house, and which to the servant quarters.

Charles Cameron opened the correct door and sent her in the right direction, then turned to Sean. His expression wasn't pleased. Wasn't anything near to pleased. "A word with you, Baldwin?"

Sean nodded. "Lead the way."

He stripped the knot in his tie and walked off in the direction of his study. Sean followed him in and went directly to the phone on Cameron's desk, lifted the receiver and punched in the code to ring estate security. Cameron switched on a recessed light over the wetbar and poured himself a shot of brandy. The only other light in the room came from a brass library lamp beside the phone.

Someone picked up the call. "Clement Basye, Dr. Cameron."

"This is Baldwin," Sean corrected him. "In Cameron's study. Anything happen after we left?"

"Nothing."

"The cameras are all in operation?"

"Yes," Basye answered. "Nothing going down at all."

Sean nodded and disconnected. Cameron settled into the large oxblood leather executive chair behind his desk and gestured at Sean to be seated.

He stripped out of his tux coat, loosened his own tie and sank into a matching leather chair opposite Cameron.

"I'd like," he said, leaning back in his chair, letting it swivel slowly from side to side, "to compliment you on a job well done. Your handling of the security arrangements at the hotel was first rate. Your improvisation after the surveillance cameras failed was inspired. And of course, we all got through it safe and sound." He cracked a smile. "Count Dracula notwithstanding."

Sean mirrored what seemed to him nothing more than a mocking excuse for a smile. "I hear a 'but' coming."

Cameron shrugged. "But," he obliged, "I would like to know what is going on between you and my wife."

Sean blinked. "I'm not sure I know what you're talking about."

"Oh, I have the feeling that you do, Mr. Baldwin."

Sean had the feeling Cameron was toying with him. "Enlighten me."

"You don't like Liv very much, do you?"

"I don't know her."

"That wasn't my question."

"But it is my answer."

"Come now, Mr. Baldwin, let's be frank. The neurons of the human species are all wired in more or less identical pathways. They fire themselves up without our even thinking about it. We all know at an intuitive level within the first seven or so seconds of meeting another person whether we like or dislike him. Or her. So tell me. Which is it?"

"All right. I disliked your wife on sight."

Cameron nodded thoughtfully. He picked up an expensive-looking pipe by its stem from the crystal ashtray on his desk and tapped the bowl in his palm. "Such is often the case when one finds one's libido leading."

Sean shook his head in disbelief. "You know what, Cameron? I like you even less."

Cameron laughed heartily. "Touché. I have to say, of course, that there would be cause for concern if you weren't . . . attracted to Liv."

"So what? A duel to the death?"

"An admission of guilt? Libido leading? My, my, my." Cameron's smile vanished. "But dueling with you would be rather stupid of me, now, wouldn't it?"

Sean shrugged. "Name a second."

Cameron laughed again, this time with a more genuine tenor. "We might find we like each other after all, Baldwin. But of course, it's irrelevant—isn't it?—so long as you're doing what you were brought here to do."

"Supposing I agree to stay on."

Cameron's face darkened. "What is that supposed to mean?"

"It means I'm out of here unless you start filling me in on the salient details."

"I don't know what you mean."

"I have the feeling, sir," Sean cracked in Cameron's own contemptuous voice, "that you do."

Cameron sat back. "Enlighten me."

"Tell you what you already know?" Sean asked. "Your wife is a basket case."

"How observant of you." Cameron sighed. "She's been under a terrible strain—"

"So she says."

"My God, man, she's frightened of her own shadow, and not without reason—"

"But then," Sean interrupted, "she can't seem to recall being there when her last bodyguard bled to death all over her."

Cameron grimaced. "A deficiency you corrected, I suppose?" He didn't wait for Sean's answer. "Do you have any idea of the psychological damage you might have inflicted?"

Again, he went on without waiting for an answer. "You may be the best at what you do, Baldwin. I'm assured that you are, and I'm counting on it. But let me make myself perfectly clear. Your job is to protect her life, and I will not tolerate you running roughshod over whatever mental or emotional defenses she has constructed to save her own sanity."

Sean got up and adjusted his shoulder holster, then stuck an arm in his tux coat.

"What are you doing?" Cameron demanded angrily.

"It's very late. I'm turning in for the night, Cameron. But I'll be leaving as soon as Protection, Inc. can send in a replacement."

"Now you listen just one goddamned minute, Baldwin—"

"No, *you* listen," Sean retorted, jabbing a finger at Cameron. "I don't like you, it's true. I don't like the setup, and I don't much care for your wife. You'd have to know me better to know that's not my usual. How long have you lived here?"

"Seven years—"

"Seven."

"That's right. Seven years."

"Then don't ask me to swallow stress and emotional upset for the reason your wife can't remember the way into this house. It sticks in my craw, Cameron."

"There are reasons . . . the press—" Cameron complained.

"Fine. Really. Have it your way. I understand. But I don't give a damn about what you're trying to keep out of the tabloids. If I don't know what's going on, if I don't get to hear the truth, then I can't—no, make that *won't*—be responsible for your wife's life."

Cameron's jaw tightened. "You're quite right, I think. We're not going to like each other. But you're the best. I need the best. Liv needs you."

"I understand, Cameron. I just don't sympathize. You can either let me in on the full extent of her problems and the threats against her, and do it now, or you can find yourself whoever the hell is second best."

"Now is hardly the time," Cameron snapped. "It's nearly three-thirty in the morning."

"The choice is yours."

He sighed heavily. "I don't know where to start."

Sean stood there waiting for an answer, but the good doctor was spared trying to come up with a start to the truth. In the same moment, like a house of cards slipping away one by one, estate security called, Clement Basye announced a "serious problem" over Cameron's speakerphone, and his wife burst into the room.

"Dr. Cameron, sir," Basye's voice asked, "is your wife there with you?"

His attention scattershot, Cameron stared at the speakerphone, and then at his wife, who was still wearing the jeans and U.C. Irvine sweatshirt she'd changed into to return home.

Sean thought, then, about the improbability of an Olivia Simons Cameron possessing a University of California sweatshirt. She couldn't catch her breath, and Sean decided his being here with Cameron was a nasty shock to her.

"Liv?" Cameron answered Basye, eyeing her. "Yes. She's right here."

"Thank God. We thought—"

"No—" she interrupted, her body language begging Cameron to listen to her. "Please—"

"What?" Cameron barked, though at her or Basye, Sean couldn't have said.

"They—"

"Sir, we thought she was missing from her quarters. Sachi is nowhere to be found."

Sean's amazement just kept feeding on itself. "Sachi?"

"Olivia's basset hound," she explained. "But—" The look on Sean's face stopped her cold, but Cameron just went barreling on.

"So what the bloody hell is that supposed to mean?" he demanded, glaring at Sean and then at the woman who was supposed to be his wife. "That stupid bitch is too inbred and feeble-brained to find her way out to the lawn and back. Olivia probably took her—"

"But she didn't—I mean, Olivia isn't outside with Sachi. At least, nowhere any of the estate guards have searched." Abbie locked stares a moment with Sean, then swallowed hard and spoke directly to Cameron. "Dr. Cameron, Olivia is nowhere to be found."

"Impossible." Cameron launched himself out of his chair and sent the pipe he'd been fondling crashing into the crystal ashtray. "Find her," he snapped at the speakerphone.

"Sir," Basye's voice protested, "we are trying, but I'd estimate that we've searched over eighty percent of the estate. Your wife—"

"Then I suggest," Cameron ordered softly, "that you cover the other twenty percent." He stabbed the button to disconnect, then turned away and dragged a hand through his thick graying hair.

Sean folded his arms and sat on Cameron's desk, one thigh perched, the other leg bracing him. He knew now, sooner than Abbie ever imagined, that the woman who stood before him was not Olivia. That he'd been lied to repeatedly. That she was not his employer's wife.

Not anyone's wife.

He'd been toyed with on a professional level and lied to by her on another. But Olivia was missing and Abbie couldn't think about might-have-beens between her and Sean. She folded her arms, too, and stood there feeling sick for Charles Cameron's sake.

He sighed heavily. "All right, Baldwin. There you have it. The truth, the whole truth. This is Abbie Callahan. She is acting as my wife's double until the threats against Olivia's life have been stopped. Are you satisfied?"

"No." Sean angled his head. "But it answers all my problems with this little charade tonight. The rest can wait." He looked at Abbie. "But you've got a real problem if Abbie here—and the estate security—are to be believed. The real Olivia Cameron is now missing."

"And gone where, exactly?" Cameron demanded angrily. "Do you imagine on an estate as well guarded as this she can have simply disappeared?"

"I'm not imagining anything, Cameron. You, on the other hand, are delusional if you think that on the other twenty percent of the estate—the gardening shed for instance, or the dog run, or the bottom of the duck pond for that matter—"

"Do you have to be so crude?" Abbie snapped.

"That your wife is likely to be found," Sean finished calmly.

Every vestige of color drained from Cameron's face. He collapsed in his chair as if he were a marionette and the strings had just been severed. "Dear God, what if he's snatched her?"

Snatched her? Abbie shoved her hair out of her face. "Who?"

"Whoever the hell is trying to kill her! What if he snatched her instead?"

Sean frowned. "You think this is a kidnapping?"

"If I knew what to think this was," Cameron muttered incoherently, unable even to focus his eyes. He stood again and tore around the desk. "I've got to find her. I've got to help her. She's out there alone or—"

"Wait." Sean caught his arm.

"No," he shouted, his eyes wide with panic. "She needs me now—"

"Get a hold of yourself," Sean commanded. "Just stop and think a minute. She'll need you when they find her, but you have half a dozen trained men out there searching for her."

He jerked his arm free. "If they were *trained*," he snarled, tears shining fiercely in his eyes, "she wouldn't be missing, now would she?"

Abbie clapped a hand over her mouth to keep from crying out. "Dr. Cameron, he's right. Maybe if you just try to stay calm, you can think—"

"Was it you who found her gone?" Cameron railed, turning on Abbie. She took an involuntary step back. Cameron moved forward accusingly. "Was it?"

"Watch yourself, Cameron," Sean warned.

"Will you just shut up!" she cried. "Can't you see he's destroyed by this?" She turned back to Cameron. "To answer your question, yes. I... The lights were on in her suite. I could see that. I thought she'd want to know what an incredible success her charity ball had been."

Cameron's tension had the veins popping up in his neck and face. He pressed the knuckles of one hand to his temple. "Go on."

"I knocked. She didn't answer the door. I thought I would at least hear Sachi whining like she always does, but I didn't hear a sound. I just got this awful feeling inside, so I went in."

Cameron's brow creased deeply. "Her door was unlocked?"

"Yes."

Cameron shook his head, but the movements were so small he looked almost palsied. "I don't understand." He moved, trancelike, back around his desk and sank into his chair again.

Abbie's chest tightened. Sean didn't look amused. She exchanged glances with him, aware that on a subtle level everything between them had shifted. He held her glance, but not from anything other than the gravity of the situation. She had to respect him for that.

She turned to Cameron. "If you believe Olivia's been kidnapped, shouldn't we call the police?" Abbie asked.

Cameron clinched his fists, fighting to stay in control of himself. "Fine. Do it."

Sean let out a frustrated breath. Leaning on Cameron's desk again, he punched up the security office on the speakerphone.

Basye came on in a harried voice.

"I take it you haven't found Mrs. Cameron?" Sean asked.

"No sign of her. None at all. Her patio door was unlocked, and the dog *is* gone. Her maid, Jessica, says there are no suitcases or clothes missing. We'll keep—" He broke off to answer the rattling sound of a radio call. Abbie held her breath. Cameron closed his eyes, praying she thought, for an answer, for his wife to be found safe and sound.

But when Basye came back on, they each knew better. "I'm coming up."

"What is it?" Sean demanded.

"Be right there."

Cameron got out of his chair and paced behind his desk. His jaw was clamped shut. He couldn't find anything to do with his hands. Sick with fear for Olivia and sympathy for Charles Cameron, Abbie just wanted to throw up and be done with it.

Basye came into the room looking like hell, like a man anticipating his head on the chopping block. "The, uh . . . the back gate on the south end is hanging open. I'm told they can't be sure if only one person came through, and left, or two—whatever, and the . . . Sachi."

Abbie couldn't speak for the shock, nor could Cameron. Sean took up the slack. "The south rear gate is literally hanging open?"

"Yes."

"And the cameras didn't pick this up?"

Basye gulped and cleared his throat. "The construction equipment for the new stone fence blocks the camera."

Sean swore under his breath. "You're certain someone went through the gate at all?"

"The turf is very wet, so, yes. It's lightly trampled. I'm told it looks as if the someone came up from or went down to the boat launch. Or both."

Abbie swallowed hard. "We should get the police here before any more time passes—"

"Or the guards obscure whatever leads there are," Sean agreed.

"Dear God," Cameron murmured, stricken. "I— I'm not sure we should call in the police—"

"I am," Sean snapped, punching up the speakerphone again.

"No . . . Listen to me!" Cameron insisted.

Sean stared at him. "Your *wife* is *missing*. How much more reason do you need?"

Cameron gritted his teeth, then dismissed Basye with orders to have the grounds searched one more time, concentrating on the boathouse and launch. He waited until Basye had gone, then wiped his eyes with a handkerchief. "There is another possibility here."

"Other than kidnapping you mean?"

Cameron nodded shakily. "I believe ... I believe Olivia may have finally cracked under the pressure."

"Go on," Sean ordered. Abbie thought he could have taken a more empathetic tone.

"The back gate cannot be opened from the outside."

"Unless," Abbie suggested, "someone from the outside made it over the top."

"But then the alarms would have had to fail—" Sean broke off and stood. "Tell me the alarms aren't on the same circuit as the cameras."

Cameron shook his head. "I don't know. I leave those details to the experts. But if they are, then ... what?"

"Then," Sean explained painstakingly, "in the time it took to get the breaker restored, someone could have come over the fence and security would never be the wiser."

Cameron gulped. "I hadn't thought of that."

Sean reached for the speakerphone again.

"Wait," Abbie objected. "Just a minute." She turned to Cameron. "What was the point you were going to make?"

Cameron flashed her a grateful look, then shook his head as if he couldn't believe what he was about to say. Outside the pool of light cast by the small, powerful library lamp, his shadowed features twisted in pain. "I believe . . . that is, I think it's a strong possibility that Liv. . . escaped. Um, ran away."

"Escaped?" Sean asked, astonished.

"No!" Abbie protested. "Why would she do that?"

"Because in her heart she believed no one could protect her."

"But the fence, the stone fence you're building—"

"Didn't matter." Cameron shook his head. "Didn't matter. She's battled these excessive fears since childhood. Oswald killed Jack Kennedy on Liv's twelfth birthday. Bobby Kennedy was murdered the day she graduated from Marymount. Some crack-brained palm reader once told her she would die young and a martyr." Cameron's chin trembled. "Fated to die. She joked about it for years, but it isn't a joke any longer."

"Had she given you any indication that she would bolt?" Sean asked.

"Never directly. But I know her, inside and out. I could *feel* it. She believed she was never going to be safe here again."

"Do you have anything more substantial than a feeling, Cameron?"

"Yes." Cameron shot him a withering look. "Her last, late bodyguard."

"Tensley?" Sean asked.

Cameron jerked his head toward Sean. "I thought you people didn't know each other. I was guaranteed complete anonymity between bodyguards—"

"What did he know?" Sean interrupted, ignoring the issue of the Protection Services, Inc. guarantee.

"I don't know what he knew," Cameron retorted. "What I do know is that Tensley's last words were, 'Tell her,' 'not' and 'run.' "

Abbie's insides turned cold. The images in the videotape Cameron had shown her took on deadly significance if Tensley's last words meant what Cameron assumed. Olivia had been angry and arguing with him when he was shot and killed. "Maybe she had asked him for help?"

"He would have refused," Sean said.

Cameron's lips trembled. "Yes. I'm sure that's the case."

Sean drew a deep breath. "If this place was what she feared, Cameron, why didn't you just take your wife away from here?"

"It wasn't only this place. It wouldn't have mattered where she was. Liv was beyond paranoid. I could have taken her anywhere on earth—and sacrificed the protection I could provide here—but it *wouldn't have mattered*. I thought she'd begun to see that." He turned to face Abbie. "It was originally Liv's idea to find a double for her."

Abbie frowned. "Didn't you tell me she was opposed to the idea?"

"That's what I'm trying to tell you. From one week to the next, one *day* to the next, she changed her mind. She'd lost all ability to discriminate among her choices. She couldn't arrive at a decision. She was in a state of shock that wouldn't resolve itself. Liv was incapable of carrying through with anything."

Sean stood. "You're lying through your caps, Cameron, or else you're a fool."

Stunned by Sean's hostile affront, Cameron ceased to move or breathe. His voice shook in anger. "I beg your pardon."

Abbie knew how he felt. Exactly. "Do you have any idea who you're talking to?" she demanded. "Dr. Cameron is a world-renowned psychiatrist—"

"Bull." Sean interrupted, ruthlessly cutting Abbie off, getting in Cameron's face. "Either your wife left this estate under her own power and the noses of an entire security force, or she's incapable of putting one foot in front of the other. You can't have it both ways, Cameron."

Chapter Five

Exhausted but too keyed up to sleep, and ravenously hungry, an hour later Abbie gave up trying. She left her room and padded through the silent dark house to the kitchen to make herself an omelet and toast.

Sean Baldwin was already there, slouched in a chair in the dark. A jar of instant decaf sat open where he'd left it and the door of the microwave hung open, providing the only light in the roomy marble-floored kitchen.

Stripped of his cummerbund and coat, shoes and socks, he still wore the elegant starched shirt and slacks. The shirt was half undone. The black leather shoulder holster rested in place over wrinkles it had created.

He said nothing, only watched her. Abbie swallowed hard, switched on the overhead lights. He squinted against the harsh light. Perversely pleased to cause him any discomfort, she went to the massive black-fronted refrigerator to pull out the eggs and butter and fresh veggies for her omelet.

She'd have been fine with the silence alone, but not with him sitting there watching her searching for a bowl and whisk. Tossing about for something civil to.

say to him, she finally asked, "What happened with Dr. Cameron after I left?"

"Nothing." Sean drained his mug of the decaf he'd microwaved and set it back down. "Cameron is sticking with the runaway theory. I agreed to wait on calling the authorities at least until morning." He stared out the countless, multipaned windows into the darkness and laughed softly. "Daylight, I should say."

She refused to be charmed by a hint of humor in him. "Why did you agree to that?"

"There is no evidence of a crime. No ransom note, no forced entry, no trespass, no corpse."

No corpse. She should be getting used to his heartless characterizations. She turned to the sink and scrubbed a few scallions and perfectly formed mushrooms till they were a little ragged. "Is it true the police won't act on a missing persons report for a couple of days?"

"In most jurisdictions. They'd scrap the rules in a New York minute on Olivia Simons Cameron's name alone. But that feeds Cameron's biggest fear."

"Which is what?"

"That any report of Olivia being missing would be leaked to the press—that her father would have a stroke just hearing that kind of scoop."

"The ambassador is in very fragile health."

"You know that for yourself, or is it what you've been told?"

"It's common knowledge." She slapped the vegetables down on the marble cutting board. "Do you doubt that kind of news would upset any father?"

"What kind of news? All we know is that she's gone. Maybe the only thing that's gone down tonight is that Olivia Cameron walked out on her husband when she knew he wouldn't be looking. For that matter, the ambassador might even be heartened to know she's *escaped.*"

Abbie's head jerked up. Cameron had used that term, and Sean wasn't letting it drop. "I don't believe you! I can't even believe you called Dr. Cameron a liar. Do you have a grasp at all on the concept of compassion?"

"Yeah. I save it for widows and orphans. Mitch Tensley had a wife and two little kids. Boys. Think they're going to miss their dad?"

Abbie sent him a scathing look, then returned to hacking away at the small stack of scallions on the marble cutting board. "I didn't know that he had children—but I know exactly how they'll miss him. You, on the other hand, don't have the slightest idea how deeply in love with his wife Charles Cameron is, or how frantic over what's become of her. Do you have a clue what it's like to love someone like that?"

"Nope. You do?"

The knife came way too close to her finger. She slowed her chopping, then halted altogether. She met his look. "I know it when I see it."

"Yeah?"

"Yeah."

"Well, sweetheart, I know a liar when I see one, too."

She scraped the scallions into a frying pan. "You offend me on so many levels, I don't even know how to tell you. Do *not* call me sweetheart—and don't presume to judge Dr. Cameron. If you had one tenth the integrity that man has in his little finger—"

"Stow it, Abbie. If Charles Cameron had the kind of principles you're fantasizing, he would have told me up front about this little scheme he cooked up to have you double for his wife."

She cracked three shells, one by one, and let the raw eggs plop into a small mixing bowl. She began to beat them. "That might have been a poor judgment call—"

"Might have been? Lady—"

"Abbie. Not sweetheart, not *lady*. Why don't you just make it Ms. Callahan?"

"Abbie, then." He shut his eyes and massaged them with a thumb and forefinger, then looked longingly at her omelet preparations. "How much groveling would it take to get you to make me one of those, too?"

The bowl nearly slipped from her hand into the omelet pan with the eggs. "More than you're capable of."

Smiling to himself, he looked down, then back up at her from beneath his strong, masculine brow. "You might be surprised. Hunger makes a man..."

"Tractable?" she supplied, rolling the pan to spread the eggs.

He eyed her. "More."

Heat climbed in her. She put the pan down before it slipped from her grasp. "I don't know what that means."

He breathed heavily. His chest rose and fell. For a moment she couldn't stop seeing the stark white shirt placket open against his curling dark chest hairs.

"Look, Abbie. We're on the same side here. You might try to remember that."

She ran a spatula around the edge of the omelet, more to take her focus from him than anything else. "Which side would that be?" she gibed, spreading sliced mushrooms over the cooking eggs. "Surely not Dr. Cameron's."

"His wife's. But it's the middle of the night. I'm hungry and—"

"Helpless?"

"Prickly, aren't we?" His lips quirked in a sideways smile. "But frankly, yes. I don't boil water well." He clapped his mouth shut, then spoke again. "I'd rather be friends than enemies, Abbie, and I could use something to eat. That's all."

What he managed well, she thought, was plundering her anger at him without ever seeming the least bit sorry for harsh judgments, from her role to Cameron's silence on the subject. Judgments he had no business making.

But the fair streak in her lobbied that he did have the right to question anything. Everything. To know in minute detail what he should know to protect his client. For all Abbie knew, she was only still alive courtesy of the judgment calls in security Sean Baldwin had made tonight.

And if he were with Olivia Cameron right now, wherever she was, instead of with Abbie, Olivia would be safe.

He wasn't. He was here with her, sitting bare-footed and nearly bare-chested in a kitchen alone with her, and he was hungry.

"Can you get your own vegetables? Or there's a really wonderful baby Swiss cheese in the refrigerator."

He smiled. "I could handle that."

"Okay. You grate, I'll eat." She slipped her omelet from the pan onto a plate, poured herself a glass of wine and sat down. He hadn't moved. "You can grate cheese?"

"Probably." He shrugged. "I made a pizza from a box once. Big mistake. I bought that stuff that was already grated."

Abbie swallowed a bite of her omelet and gave a wry smile. He had a way of reducing her tension, making her feel important and happy to volunteer to do it for him—and all in a way that dazzled her because she didn't resent any of it. "Never mind. If you don't mind waiting until I finish, I'll do it."

"I can wash the dishes," he offered.

"Valiant," Abbie observed, "but there's a dishwasher and kitchen help with not a lot else to do."

He shrugged. "Okay." He turned more fully toward her, planting his forearms on the table. "Abbie, I could use some insider information here."

"I'm not much of an insider. I've been here less than a week." She cut the last piece of her omelet into two. "How can I help?"

"Just be as straightforward as you know how to be."

His look was pointed, almost an accusation without being one. A shame, really. Her friend Bibi could have told him. He would have to know her a very long time for her to tell him anything that really mattered. And if he thought he had her loyalty over Charles Cameron, he was wrong. Even if his efforts had prevented an attempt on her life at the charity ball, he was only doing his job, not some personal favor to her that meant she ought to spill everything she knew.

But she could play it his way for now, tell him what he needed to know. "Okay. I'll give you 'straightforward.'

"My name is Abbie Callahan, not Abigail. I'm a native Californian. I'm a writer and make a decent living as what the studios call a script doctor. I met Charles Cameron briefly a few years ago. My resemblance to his wife was striking enough that when he began to look for a double for Olivia, he thought of me. As I understand it, he asked Delia Barry to find me and fly me to New York.''

"Then he convinced you to be Olivia's public persona.''

"Yes.''

"Didn't it seem too close to playing the innocent lamb all staked out, baiting the predator in?''

Not wanting to dwell on that aspect of her commitment, she started to get up to fix his omelet.

He reached out and covered her hand, making it impossible for her to get up without answering him first. "Abbie. Why did you agree to pose as Olivia?''

She stared at him, anxious again. All that flattery and tension-diffusing job he'd done on her was wasted now. "Is there no question you won't ask?''

"No.''

"Well, there are some I won't answer.''

"Which only makes me want to know more.''

"My motives have nothing to do with Olivia's disappearance tonight.'' She got up then, and rinsed her plate in the sink. He was going to let her off easy. She began cracking more eggs into the mixing bowl.

"What do you know of Cameron's motives in all this?''

"He's a man deeply in love with his wife.'' Abbie swallowed. This was getting perilously close to the important things, the reason she had agreed in the first place. She felt defiant of her own need to hold back. "I admire that very much.''

"You want it for yourself,'' he guessed.

"Someday." She turned to get the imported Swiss from the refrigerator, then spent a few seconds finding a grater. "With the right man."

His eyes followed her hands. "Who will that be, Abbie Callahan?"

Heat filled her chest. "A man's man. Someone who would leap into the fray for me. Someone to open doors for me or throw himself in front of speeding bullets." She knew, and he knew she knew, he was one of those. She could see it in his eyes. The thing that remained to be seen was if he would do those things for her. For Abbie Callahan.

And if he was really the one she wanted to be doing them for her.

Her chin lifted. "Someone like your friend Mitch Tensley."

Sean let the silence draw out.

"Or someone like Charles Cameron?" He said at last. "He's fronting a lot of money, but I can't quite see him dodging bullets for his beloved Olivia."

She didn't understand Sean. Cameron was doing everything under the sun for his wife's peace of mind. More. But of course, as her personal bodyguard, and one who had never lost a client, Sean would consider Olivia's peace of mind a given. Only her physical safety concerned him.

More, she didn't understand his attitude. "Why do you dislike Charles Cameron so much?" *Or me*, she thought.

"I don't trust him."

Or me? "Why not? He's—"

"What he's done is hold back essential information, and he hasn't improved on his record tonight." He looked directly into her eyes. "You're holding back, Abbie Callahan. What is it driving you? Some noble idea of taking a stand against evil?'' His question blew her away, and he just went on as if he'd been privy to her secret heart, her reasoning for plunging ahead into Olivia Cameron's threatened life. ''Whose standard of right and wrong are you trying to live up to?''

''My own,'' she snapped.

His eyes narrowed. ''But, of course, you were raised that way weren't you? What were your parents?''

''Missionaries,'' she cracked.

His hearty masculine laugh plucked her feminine nerves like a concert cellist at his E string.

But she was unnerved again at his insight—his intrusion, really, into her privacy. She poured beaten eggs into the skillet and rolled it, then diced a few fresh scallions. ''My mother was a bookkeeper for an insurance company. My dad was a beat cop.''

''Killed in the line of duty?''

''Yes.'' She imagined if all she'd ever said to Sean Baldwin was hello, he'd have read her life's history into it. Of course she'd admitted to knowing exactly how Mitch Tensley's kids would feel, but she felt flattered by his intense interest again, and faked out of information she would have sworn she would not spill to him.

''How old were you? Eight? Nine?''

''Twelve. Old enough to believe what my daddy told me was important. I *was* raised that way. You don't often get a chance in life to stand up and be counted.''

She wanted the glint she saw in his eyes to be admiration. She wanted it too much. She popped halves of an English muffin into the toaster. To distract him, she went on with the straightforward facts she'd intended him to have.

"Cameron asked me to pose as Olivia in public situations where her presence is expected. He told me she despised the idea, but that he needed time to flush out whoever it is that murdered her brother, attacked her father, killed her bodyguard and continues to threaten her.

"So, yes." She stopped, poured more of the dry fruity wine and took a sip for courage, then sprinkled cheese on the omelet and turned half of it over on itself. "I held out on you. I did everything I could to make you believe I was Olivia."

"Because Cameron wanted it that way?"

"For one thing." Slipping the omelet neatly from the pan to a plate, she nodded in agreement, then spread the toasted English muffin with cloves of baked garlic.

"What else?"

She noticed he was buttoning up his shirt to be more proper at the table. She flashed him an approving smile, then served the plate along with cutlery and a linen napkin and sat down again herself. "I thought if I could be convincing to you as Charles Cameron's wife, then I might have a prayer of bringing off the charity ball in her stead."

He plowed into the omelet, then the English muffin spread with garlic. "Wow. Abbie, this is really fine."

"I'm glad you like it, but you're probably so hungry I could have heated up a can of Sachi's designer dog food."

He laughed again. "No." He shook his head and downed another couple of bites. "It wouldn't have been the same at all. How did you learn to cook like this?"

She put her chin into her hand. "Therapy."

"For what?"

"Writing is tough, you know? Never ending. You're never quite done with it. There are always ways to improve on a scene or a character even when you have finished. But it's such a long haul getting from beginning to end that you wind up looking for something you can do well and be done with in an hour or two." She shrugged, vastly pleased at his pleasure in her efforts. "Cooking is my path to immediate gratification."

"Lucky me."

She smiled. "I have lots of friends who appreciate me, too."

"I'll bet." He grinned. Drank wine. Looked at her. Drank more. "Count me in."

She had the feeling the last thing he wanted was to feel anything more for her than he would for any of his friends, but he was drawn to her.

She was drawn to him. The chemistry was burning up the oxygen between them.

She didn't need another friend, and the last thing she wanted was a man's man like him making her into a buddy.

She wasn't going to play Lois to his Clark. She wanted the real thing or nothing at all, thank you. "So. Are you saying I wasn't convincing as Olivia?"

He pushed his plate aside, having scraped up every morsel. "You were, Abbie. I just hope you can be as convincing when we see Ambassador Simons later this morning."

Chapter Six

Ambassador Simons lived alone on an estate little more than a stone's throw from the one Charles Cameron had bought for his wife. Approaching eighty, half blinded by inoperable cataracts, spiritually bereft after the murder of his son Peter, the ambassador had been confined to a wheelchair since the attack of an intruder seven weeks before.

Abbie couldn't imagine fooling the canny old man despite his many infirmities. If he were blind and deaf, surely he would know his own daughter. But Charles Cameron believed that if Abbie smelled like his daughter, bathed and shampooed with her toiletries and dressed in clothes belonging to Olivia, the only way the ambassador would know she was a fake was if Olivia had turned up at his estate seeking refuge in the only place she had ever felt safe.

There were only three scenarios. Olivia might have run to her father's estate. She might have run elsewhere with his backing and help. Worst case, she had been kidnapped, or was already dead.

The ruse Charles Cameron conceived was meant to protect the fragile old man from the devastating possibility of the real harm to his sole remaining offspring. The hope was that Olivia had run to her father's safekeeping in some desperate childish belief that if anyone could keep her safe from harm, it would be her daddy.

Cameron believed it was possible the old man had given his daughter refuge in some ill-conceived attempt to hide her away from a very dangerous world, even if that meant concealing her whereabouts from Cameron himself. Sean wasn't buying. He sat in Olivia Cameron's sitting room on a chair built for a woman, at the phone on an antique Belgian desk that suited a woman's space. He could hear Abbie Callahan humming softly in the shower, the Beatles' tune that went with "spread your broken wings and learn to fly," over and over again till he wanted to bellow into her the rest of the damned song.

But he wouldn't.

He was too aware of her purpose, of Abbie Callahan coating her thin, feminine body with the soaps and oils and scents of Olivia Simons Cameron.

He'd agreed in principle to spare her father any potentially devastating news of Olivia's disappearance until they could find out what had become of his daughter. But in the meantime, this was Sean's lot.

He'd slept for a couple of hours, then spent the last few calling on friends. He wanted the phone records to find out what calls had come into or out of the Cameron estate in the last eight weeks. His buddy in the computer archives at the Maryland phone company was prepared to cough up to Sean what would take anyone else a court order to get.

He wanted the police reports on the investigation of the murder of Peter Simons, and the ones on file in the attack on the ambassador seven weeks before. A high-level commander in the D.C. police department pulled the records on the Simons murder, and greased the way for Sean to get copies of records under seal in the case of the ambassador himself.

He wanted the impressions of the media types who'd covered the murder on Peter and the unreported assault on the ambassador, but his friend at the *Post* was out.

Sean wasn't worried. He'd find a way to connect. He always did. He knew what people needed; he was there, far more often than not, to provide whatever that turned out to be. He didn't do any of it to bank favors. He cared about people. He cared about helping them. In return, there wasn't a man or woman he knew who wouldn't bend over backward to help him.

Phone records and police reports constituted bending over way backward. So was the omelet Abbie Callahan had concocted for him. He'd never had baked garlic spread on an English muffin, either. He wasn't taking it for a partnership signed, sealed and delivered. She still clearly trusted Charles Cameron over Sean, but even that he respected.

He heard the water stop and then he could hear better her humming her spread-your-wings refrain. The woman had him feeling tongue-tied. He didn't like it. She was more female in a complicated, womanly fashion—and in subtly sexual ways—than he remembered ever in his life confronting, from the way she cracked eggs into a bowl to how she rested her pointed little chin in her hand.

The way her bottom swayed. Nothing deliberately provocative, so all the more so.

The way her eyes tracked him and darted away and met his look again when he least expected it.

What touched him most was her wide-eyed admiration for the impressive range of people he called friends. Friends who knew if he asked for something, there were important reasons.

But her feminine instinct to help ran so deep she was apparently willing to bet her life on it, and nothing could have been better calculated to snag Sean's powerful interest. Hers wasn't the I-am-woman-hear-me-roar, in-your-face bravado he'd seen in female cops and bodyguards. No, she was just there in the trenches willing to do what had to be done—even if that meant baiting a murderer. So to Sean, she represented this kind of Chinese puzzle he wanted to take apart.

He'd been accused straight-out, in Charles Cameron's shrewd, calculating way, of lusting after his wife. Sean didn't like that, either, even when it turned out Abbie Callahan did not belong to Cameron. The fact that Cameron recognized Sean's attraction set his teeth on edge. Either he was so ga-ga over the woman as to be witless on the subject of his own behavior around her, or Cameron was dangerously insightful.

Sean didn't want to believe either theory.

Regardless, he'd needed a wake-up call. Cameron was no fool. Unless Sean backed way off where Abbie Callahan was concerned, his vaunted edge would crumble.

He heard the blow-dryer come on. She'd picked up on another phrase to hum, the melody beneath the words, "all your life, you were only waiting for this moment to arrive."

Too bad he knew all the words. Sean got up so fast he knocked over the chair meant for a woman. Too bad the sentiment hit so close to home, too.

ABBIE, with Sean beside her, drove Olivia's Infiniti, waved at the security guard at the gate in the breezy manner Charles Cameron had described, and greeted the ambassador's household help as if they were the closest things to family she had ever known.

For Olivia Simons Cameron, Miri and Carl Bockoven were just that, the forces of constancy in a life of boarding schools and vacations and spring breaks from college when the ambassador was off in Europe or the Middle East or the Communist block knocking out one diplomatic coup after another. But for the rare vacations together, the ambassador had sacrificed a meaningful family life, and his regrets in this made his memoirs all the more poignant.

But Miri Bockoven was less than friendly, and definitely suspicious of Abbie, just as Charles Cameron had predicted. Miri ran the ambassador's life and house like a commando, and she had been a good deal less than thrilled in recent years with Olivia's infrequent visits to her father. Carl Bockoven, on the other hand, would do anything for Olivia. Anything at all, even after the years of what his wife characterized as Olivia's neglect.

Abbie had been coached to return Miri's hostility with tolerance, to use every nuance of Olivia's behavior Cameron had taught her. Cameron had described the relationship between the two women as bordering on a love-hate seesaw, but Olivia would never have tried to curry favor. Instead, so long as Miri performed her duties on the estate of her father, Olivia tolerated her anger.

Miri's general hostility made it impossible to tell, though, if Olivia had fled here and Miri Bockoven was hiding the fact.

She directed Abbie and Sean to the south lawn. They found the ambassador, Olivia's father, parked in his wheelchair at the edge of a duck pond on his estate, a mohair blanket covering his legs. In his lap were pieces of gourmet croissants, but he'd been dozing. The waddling ducks weren't quite hungry enough to nip at his blanket, reminding him to scatter the crumbs.

He startled awake at Abbie's gentle touch. "Daddy? It's me, Liv. Were you just snoozing away?"

Sean had warned her. She was not dealing with any elderly man, but rather a canny, worldly wise, hard-nosed, soft-spoken, big-stick-carrying diplomat, and she should not be fooled by whatever visage he chose to reveal. The disorientation she saw in his rheumy gray eyes was not to be believed, but Abbie was still charmed by the pleasure in his smile.

"Liv?" He looked up, squinting against the sunlight streaming through winter-bared tree branches. "Is it you, my sweet? How long has it been?"

Tufts of snow-white hair stuck out above his ears and in a fringe around the back of his head, but otherwise, age spots mottled the skin covering the top of his head. Abbie thought of her own dad, whose abundant hair would have thinned but never left him bald.

Emotion swamped her, long-ago feelings of loss. She rested her cheek against the ambassador's head and hugged his narrow, wasted shoulders. She was greeting one of the nation's most highly treasured statesmen, a true gentleman, as his daughter, and the charade shamed her.

"It's me, Daddy." She exchanged glances with Sean. It felt obvious to her that Ambassador Simons had not seen or heard from Olivia in days or weeks. "I can't think how long it's been, but I'm here now."

"You've time to sit and talk awhile?"

She nodded. "I do, yes."

The ambassador looked past her. "Who is this?"

Abbie stood aside. "Daddy, I'd like you to meet my bodyguard, Sean Baldwin. He wanted to meet you, and then go back up to the house to talk to Miri and Carl. Sean, this is my father, the honorable Ambassador Avery Simons."

Sean stepped nearer the wheelchair and held out his hand. "Sir. I'm very honored to meet you."

"And I, you." The ambassador stuck out a thin, liver-spotted hand. Abbie could see Sean was impressed by the strength of the old man's grip. "You're new."

Sean nodded. "Yes."

"Why? Where's Tensley?"

That he knew Tensley's name surprised Abbie, but the ambassador had been spared the news of Mitch Tensley's death while protecting Olivia. Sean thought the old man could handle the news—that in fact, a man of Ambassador Simons's strength and character and sensibilities would far rather confront the truth than be protected from it like a helpless man unable to tolerate the harsh realities of life.

Simons had gone head-to-head at the negotiating table with some of the most intimidating, powerful, unstable men in the world. He wouldn't crumble in the face of threats to Olivia's life. He simply wouldn't know how to fall to pieces. It wasn't in his constitution.

Sean deferred to Abbie. They had agreed to be as truthful as possible in the midst of lying to the ambassador.

"Mitch was killed, Daddy. A couple of weeks ago, protecting me." Sean sketched the important details of the assault from the river.

The ambassador seemed dumbstruck for a moment, as if, despite a lifetime of dealing with cultures and powermongers displaying less regard for human life than for their own coffers, he couldn't quite believe such an attack against his daughter. He cleared his throat. His chin wagged. Abbie could see he despised the infirmity.

"I pray yours is not the next life to be lost, Mr. Baldwin. And that you're up to the task of protecting my daughter's life."

"I'm giving it everything, sir."

The ambassador nodded. "See to it. You say you want to speak with the household staff?"

"Yes, if you have no objection."

Abbie had spread a blanket on the ground and sat holding hands with the old man. Sean sank to his haunches to meet the old man eye to eye.

"None whatever," he said. "You understand, of course, that they have been interviewed at length by the police."

"Of course. Only for background," Sean answered, "trying to get a sense of the character of the person bent on destroying your family."

The ambassador nodded tiredly. "I've made enemies in my lifetime, certainly, but retribution for whatever I've done seems belated to me, and I cannot see the logic of picking off my children, unless the purpose is to break my heart, piece by piece."

Sean breathed deeply, thoughtfully, surveying the property. It was no wonder Olivia had asked Cameron to erect a stone fence. The ambassador's property was surrounded by a wall of the rugged granite native to the northeast, in a fence twenty feet high surrounding the estate, with only the interruption of the massive wrought-iron gates at the drive. The fence had almost certainly been constructed thirty years ago when the house had been built.

"Sir, as I understand it, Peter's murder was no random act of violence. He was shot point-blank in the chest in his office to the rear of his restaurant. The obvious implication is that for the murderer to have gotten so close, Peter had to know him."

The old man nodded. "Yes." His shoulders trembled. "Whoever it was knew Peter and intended to kill him."

Sean's eyes narrowed in the same way they had when he'd accused Abbie of holding back, but he let it go.

"If you don't mind, then, I'll go off and explore a little. Talk to the Bockovens."

Abbie sat for a long while without talking, watching the ducks paddling idly along the surface of the pond.

After a while the ambassador spoke softly to her. "Are you very frightened, Liv?"

She nodded. "I am. Mitch's death was horrible. I don't know what to do, Daddy, where to go, who to trust."

"You have a great many friends, Liv. Let them help you."

But Abbie had no way of knowing which of Olivia's friends was trustworthy. "I know. But if the police are right, Peter knew his murderer. That sort of...destroys my faith. I'm tempted to...to just go away. Get away from anyone who knows me.''

The ambassador let go of her hands and tossed pieces of expensive croissants to the edge of the pond. A couple of drakes hissed and spat and snapped at each other.

''Do you remember the ranch in Colorado where we used to vacation before your mother died?'' He smiled in a far-off way. ''And the old nag you loved to ride so much?''

Abbie's breath caught. ''Yes. I loved it there.'' This was exactly the kind of information she had hoped to get, places where Olivia might have gone, where she might feel safe in going. ''What was the horse's name?''

Unsmiling, he answered. ''Buttercup.''

Sensing the trap too late, Abbie looked down at her hands. Something she'd said or done, some insignificant detail she could never have known had given her away.

The ambassador's half-blind eyes penetrated to her heart. He knew. ''The ranch was the Rocking Eight, outside of Saratoga, Wyoming. And the horse's name was Mollie.'' His expression hardened. The name of the town in Wyoming clicked in Abbie's mind because that was the name Peter Simons had given his restaurant. ''Who are you?'' the old man demanded.

''I'm sorry—''

''I've very little patience with liars, miss, and your regrets mean less than nothing to me.''

''My name is Abbie Callahan—''

''And you're impersonating my daughter because?''

He observed her struggling for something approximating the truth without exposing him to the shock of Olivia's disappearance, but she couldn't lie, not anymore. Not with any hope of gaining his help. She spotted Sean departing the house, setting off on his way down the slope to the pond.

"Ambassador Simons, I was hired by Dr. Cameron to be your daughter in public. I'm sure you know last night was the charity ball for Child Search. I was there, we were all there—"

"Including Baldwin?"

"Yes. And at least half the estate security people. Sometime during the night, Olivia . . . disappeared."

"Disappeared." His fingers knotted into fists. "Exactly what does that mean?"

"We don't know." She repeated unconsciously Sean's assessment. "There was no ransom note, no demands, no forced entry or trespassers found. And no . . . body."

Sean walked up then. Abbie knew he could see on her face that their ruse had already failed. The ambassador refused to look at him. "Did you satisfy yourself that Olivia is not hidden away in the attic?"

"Sir, yes, I did. I would have been a lot happier to find her safely here. It's my job to protect her life, but right now, I don't know where she is or if she's even alive. We had to know if she'd come here seeking refuge. I'm sorry for the deception." Abbie watched the old man making himself ease his fingers open.

"Then what you're telling me is that she escaped Cameron's clutches. I would say your obligations are over and you may both go home."

He flung the blanket high to scatter the remains of the dried croissants, then replaced the cover on his legs, jerked back on the brakes and wheeled his chair around. If she had to guess, Abbie believed that his energy would take him no farther. Sean stepped into place behind the ambassador's chair and took control before the old man would have to concede the humiliation.

Abbie snatched up the blanket she had been sitting on and scrambled to catch up with them. She gave Sean an approving look for having spared the ambassador any embarrassment, but his look warned her the old man would almost certainly hand them their heads on silver platters before he was through.

The old man took charge by the wheels after Sean shoved him up the ramp. "A chardonnay, if you please," he commanded Miri, pushing on through the kitchen, beyond the hardwood floor of the dining room and living room into his study.

The ambassador remained silent until Miri had delivered and poured his glass of chardonnay. He gestured to her to leave the bottle, over her silent protest. Sean indicated with a nod of his head that Abbie should sit. He took the leather club chair closest to the ambassador's desk.

"Sir, if you know anything about your daughter's whereabouts—"

"The last thing I would do with such information would be to share it with you."

Abbie gaped at Olivia's father. "I don't understand. Don't you want to know that she's safe?"

"If Olivia is gone from Charles Cameron's house, then she is safer than she has been in fifteen or twenty years."

Sean leaned forward, his fingers steepled between his thighs. "Sir, your daughter is in grave danger—"

"Bah! Charles Cameron is a greater threat to Olivia than a brigade of would-be assassins."

Sean sat slowly back, his expression curious, doubtful. "Ambassador Simons, I'm not a particular fan of Charles Cameron myself, but your daughter has been married to him for fifteen years. She is a force to be reckoned with in her own right, and she's represented herself to the media as an impassioned advocate of her husband. But even if things had changed between them, she had the wherewithal to get out at any time. I'm sorry, but I don't see Olivia Simons Cameron kowtowing to Cameron. To any man. She was not a victim in any sense of the word and—"

The ambassador's eyes burned with anger as he interrupted. "Charles Cameron, however, is a manipulator par excellence. Scratch his surface, and you find a psyche demented, *debilitated* by his own lack of character, by his sick need to move among the rich and powerful. He was never the man for Olivia. He is a snake whose only equal writhed in the branches of the Tree of Knowledge of Good and Evil.

"My daughter *is*," he went on, fiercely correcting Sean's use of the past tense reference to Olivia, "no saint. Yet Charles Cameron put her on a pedestal and kept her there every minute of every day. He seduced her with his power and then, when his spell began to pall, when it appeared that she wanted nothing so much as to be released from his gilded cage, he used her brother's murder to hold on to her."

Abbie felt herself wilting inside at the old man's scathing indictment of his son-in-law. "Ambassador Simons, I barely knew Olivia, but I know Dr. Cameron loves your daughter very much. How did it appear to you that he used your son's murder to hold on to her?''

"He fed her fears, made her believe only he could protect her. I can't tell you how, I only know the truth of the matter."

Abbie thought back to Cameron's own explanation of Olivia's phobias, the deaths of John and Bobby Kennedy coming at the same time as her own significant life events, the paranoia she couldn't get over that there was always going to be some kook out there determined to finish the job of wiping out a family held in high national regard, just for the fame of it. Was it possible Charles Cameron had exploited Olivia's vague, largely unrealistic fears into her full-blown anxiety disorder?

Abbie didn't believe it. The ambassador's pain was evident, but his version of the situation seemed motivated by his own pain and remorse for having sacrificed real relationships with his adult children. She felt for him, but she didn't believe he had a grip on reality in this case.

"I only know," the ambassador concluded, "that Liv was desperately unhappy, even before Peter's death."

"Because she told you as much?" Sean asked.

"No." His chin trembled again. He poured more wine and drank deeply of the chardonnay, but when he put the glass down his hand was still shaking. "I was always too harsh, too outspoken. I never accepted Liv's feelings for Cameron."

Abbie tried to make the point that this was nothing most families didn't experience. Was there ever a father who believed a man good enough for his daughter?

Simons shook his head. "This went far beyond the usual antipathy. To my mind, Charles Cameron is a man without character. A chameleon, bending and twisting and coloring himself to appear the perfect match for her."

"Isn't that the essence of love, Ambassador Simons?" Abbie asked. "That we do bend and change and color ourselves to grow, to make a marriage work, to let love evolve between us?"

Sean was staring at his hands. The ambassador sat silent for a moment. "You are an optimist by nature, Ms. Callahan. I am a realist. I've seen the worst in mankind, and I've seen the heroic, the sacrifice, the ultimate bending and twisting and coloring for the sake of peace when war seems more than justified.

"I'm telling you now," he went on, "that Cameron is a liar and an opportunist. Liv is much like you, refusing to see what is in front of your face. The conflict between us went on for many years. She had only recently begun to visit me again."

"Which is how you knew something was wrong in her life or marriage?" Sean prodded.

"Exactly so." The old man shuddered. "I knew. At first I attributed her visits to needing family after Peter's murder, but the truth was, she needed my help. I had made it impossible for Liv to admit her unhappiness to me. She was trying to find a way back. She was looking for help."

"Help in getting out?" Sean asked. "Sir, why would she need your help?"

The ambassador shrugged. "Not physical help. Emotional support, I believe." He straightened, lifting his shoulders to relieve some obscure pain. "There are only two possibilities. Either Liv was taken against her will, or she found the wherewithal, as you say, to get out from under Charles Cameron's insidious control. As the evidence lobbies in favor of the second, that is what I choose to believe. I wish her godspeed. And I urge you to leave off your search."

Sean sighed heavily. "Ambassador Simons, I respect your wishes and I hope Olivia has found some peace of mind. But none of that changes the very real fact of the threats against her life."

"Really?" the ambassador demanded sharply. "Or are these threats only the perverted lies of a madman, fabricated to bind her to him all the more?"

Sean's jaw tightened. "A man died protecting her, sir."

"A regrettable fact, to be sure—"

"A good man," Sean insisted. "A family man. The fact is, if Olivia hadn't tripped in the exact moment the gunman fired on her, she would already be dead."

"Ambassador Simons, the threats must be real—unless," Abbie whispered harshly, the thought forcing bile into her throat, "you believe that Dr. Cameron was willing for Olivia to die in that hit."

Simons's head and torso began to tremble uncontrollably. "God help me. I do."

Tears spilled from his eyes, tears of scalding regret, pain, the crushing loss of his only son and, overwhelmingly, fear for his daughter. "Charles Cameron would rather see Liv dead than free of him.

"I implore you. I beg of you. Don't find her. If you do, he will not fail again. He's lost her. She is dead to him. He will see to it that she is dead to the rest of us as well."

Chapter Seven

Sean drove Olivia's Infiniti away from Ambassador Simons's estate. Abbie used the car phone, turned on to its speakerphone mode, to check in with Charles Cameron.

He took control of the conversation before she could ask if he'd received a ransom note or any communication in their absence.

"Is Liv there at her father's estate?"

"No."

"You're certain?"

"Very much so."

His heavy sigh came clearly through the speaker.

"Dr. Cameron, your father-in-law—" Abbie broke off at Sean's warning look and, forgoing any mention of Olivia's father's powerful feelings against Cameron, continued. "Ambassador Simons is heartbroken. He didn't believe for three seconds that I was Olivia."

Another long sigh. "So you were unable to spare him news of her disappearance?"

"Yes."

"Did he have any suggestions, any possibilities for where she may have gone?"

Abbie and Sean exchanged glances. Bright midday sunlight glinted off the windshield. She wasn't one to blurt out everything she knew to anyone, but she found it very difficult with Charles Cameron. "The ambassador told us he and Olivia have not been on very good terms for many years. She wouldn't have confided in him."

"I think, Cameron," Sean added, "that you should file a missing persons report."

Cameron rejected the suggestion out of hand. "The media will be on it like vultures. The local officials won't be able to contain the case, the news will go national, the FBI will get involved . . . and the end result will be that a search for Liv will lead the assassin to within striking distance. No. I can't allow it. I forbid it." He paused only long enough to bark orders at Olivia's personal maid Jessica. "I'll see you shortly. We'll address the appropriate course of action then." He broke the connection.

"Neat twist," Sean cracked, down-shifting, pressing hard on the gas as he pulled onto the expressway.

It was clear to Abbie he wasn't going directly back to the Cameron estate. "What do you mean?"

"Simons suggests our finding Olivia will lead her murderous husband to striking distance. Cameron makes the same case, only in his version, the authorities would lead the crackpot assassin right to her. Either way, finding Olivia Cameron is a deadly proposition."

Abbie stared at him. His hands seemed way too large for the steering wheel, his legs too long despite the seat being in its furthest back position. "Surely you don't buy the ambassador's version. Dr. Cameron would no more harm a hair on Olivia's head than—"

"Get real, Abbie," Sean urged, passing car after car on the Beltway. "Your hero worship for Charles Cameron is wearing real thin. Do you honestly believe Ambassador Simons is less credible than Charles Cameron?"

"Yes, I do. He's her father and he never approved her marriage. He's guilt-ridden now, and half-deranged with grief for never being there for her—"

"According to Cameron," Sean interrupted.

"Charles Cameron has done everything humanly possible to protect Olivia—"

"And keep her terrified of her own shadow, believing only he could protect her."

"Well, she didn't buy it, did she?" Abbie said. He'd exited the Beltway into a neighborhood she wouldn't have wanted to walk alone. "Where are we going?"

"Lunch. A Thai restaurant I know of." He shot her a look. "We have to get on the same page, Ab."

She felt both chastised and encouraged. She suspected he would go to any lengths to prove her wrong, to reveal Charles Cameron for a psychopath, but Sean wasn't making everything into a pitched battle. He wanted her on the same page.

He wanted her with him.

He'd also go to any lengths to keep her at arm's length, another one of his friends. Abbie suspected a part of him wanted more. That he wanted to touch her, but it would happen when hell froze over.

Even when he broke off looking at her to concentrate on the road, she couldn't take her eyes off him. He'd worn a brown leather bomber jacket. His black hair curled softly over the collar. His profile drew her.

His commanding, aquiline nose, his lips, that jaw. Freshly shaven hours before, the shadow of stubble begged her touch.

That, too, she thought, fiercely protecting her heart, would wait for whiteout conditions in hell.

"I mean it, Abbie. The only thing we know for sure is that Olivia Cameron's life is at risk. We have to present a united front when we go back, or Cameron will find a way to thwart everything we try to do."

She managed, finally, to peel her gaze off him. "If I only agreed with you about that, we'd be a lot closer to being on the same page."

He braked for a stoplight and tilted his head. "You'll have to trust my instincts, I guess."

"What about my instincts? In the bigger picture, Cameron is simply coping with Olivia's reaction to some pretty devastating events."

Sean nodded, down-shifted and pulled into the intersection. "In a bigger picture yet, Abbie, maybe Cameron is reacting to events Olivia set in motion. If her father was right only in the most narrow sense, then Olivia wasn't happy with Cameron long before her brother was murdered or the ambassador himself was assaulted."

Abbie frowned. "Did you find out how it was possible that an intruder got onto Ambassador Simons's estate at all?"

"Possibilities, anyway. Oddly enough, the power flickered on the ambassador's estate the night the intruder got in." He looked at her. "Coincidence? I don't think so."

But he'd arrived at the hole-in-the-wall Thai restaurant, and pulled into the alley, then parked behind the crumbling redbrick establishment. "Wait for me."

He got out, whistled to an Oriental kid lurking behind the Dumpster containers and pulled a couple of bills out of a money clip.

Abbie had never seen anything like this negotiation outside of the movies. Sean was apparently dealing with the kid, handing out protection money so the car would have all its wheels and parts remaining when they got back to it.

He concluded negotiations and ruffled the kid's grimy head. He opened Abbie's door, guided her with what must have been another sort of nonverbal warning that this was his woman and not to be trifled with. She felt taken care of, cared for, even though she knew better than to make anything of it.

After she was seated in a tiny, airless room on mats on the floor, Sean went off to wash his hands.

The waiter never took his eyes off Abbie. He didn't offer a menu or water, either.

When Sean got back and sank loose-limbed to the mat opposite her, Abbie dared a whisper. "Is it dangerous to be here?"

He grinned. "Not if you're with me. But I don't come after dark myself."

Abbie shivered. "It's kind of exciting. I've never been anywhere I wouldn't go alone."

"Stick with me, kid. There are whole new vistas out there."

"Is this supposed to be some kind of bonding experience?"

He laughed. "I'm wearing off on you, Abbie Callahan. Soon there won't be any question you won't ask." He let a beat or two pass. "Is it working out that way?"

She knew he meant as a bonding experience. "Yes."

He took a drink of the alcohol the waiter had served him. The bite reflected in his look. "Good."

"Why?"

"Like I said, Abbie. We need to be working together."

She raised her brows at him. "I *meant,* why a place like this?"

"Oh. Well, to demonstrate my extensive range of knowledge and friends, of course."

"I'm impressed."

"Besides. There is no better Thai food on the planet."

"In Bangkok, surely."

He shrugged. "Chiang Rai maybe. But the owner, Mechai, walked out on the best restaurant in northern Thailand to come here."

"Why?"

"He spent many years at the mercy of the poppy-growing types in the Golden Triangle. The government has managed to shut down the borders, now, and substitute vegetable agriculture. Mechai left anyway. Too many very bad memories. In all of D.C., you won't find better Thai food."

He waited until his Thai friend, a heavy-set, dark-complexioned man with a wonderful smile, came along to help. Sean left it to the old man to choose their dishes and convey in nasal rapid-fire tones what should be brought to his American friends.

After the waiter scurried off, Mechai spoke softly, welcoming Abbie to his establishment. He barked at someone out of their sight. Sean told her he thought his old friend was warning nothing less than the finest choices should be made for their food.

"I feel sort of like Joan Wilder in *Romancing the Stone,* dropped into the middle of an adventure."

He looked at her with surprise, as if he hadn't expected her to appreciate a good adventure. Or to think of coming here as one.

She wanted very much for his interest to be personal, for his bonding experience to be more meaningful than he probably meant it to be. She couldn't think of the last time she'd actually cared. She wanted someone who wanted her more.

"Ab," he said in that way he had of consigning her to being just another name on his long, long list of friends, "why are we having this conflict?"

"Over Charles Cameron, you mean?"

"Yes."

She took a deep breath and tried to sort through her impressions of the man. "He's a brilliant man. I respect his intelligence. He has any number of high-profile clients who have endorsed him without his ever announcing to the world who he treats. And...the day he showed me the clip where your friend Mitch Tensley died, I could see a level of distress in him for Olivia's terror that just...I don't know. He touched me. I knew he loved her with all his heart."

"But in all of this, you don't see the potential for trouble? He loved her. I'm sure you're right. But what if she'd betrayed him? What if she'd begun to resent the pedestal he put her on? What if the ambassador was right? Think about it. What if Cameron's love for her evolved into an obsession neither of them could escape?"

"Sean, I don't know. I can't think how I would feel if I were Olivia under those circumstances. But don't you think you're carrying your what-ifs a little far?

Even the ambassador didn't suggest Cameron was that...obsessed.''

"Oh, I think he did." Sean waited to go on until their food had been served, then explained that her dish was chicken in a peanut sauce, his was fish done with coriander. He ate for a while, shoving food into his mouth at an impressive speed. "The point is," he said at last, "that if you don't keep an open mind, if you take everything on faith, sooner or later you'll be burned."

She wanted to know how he knew that, how he knew where to find the best Thai food, exactly how he had collected friends like Mechai. The dossier Charles Cameron had on him from Protection Services, Inc. stated that Sean had been to Thailand in the Secret Service as a bodyguard on political junkets. It was as if he soaked up every bit of information he was ever exposed to, and made friends, good, lasting friends, wherever he went.

But he was off again on the subject of taking too much on faith. "Do you know who it was, Ab, who said, 'The camera never lies, but a camera in the hand of a liar is a dangerous instrument'?"

"Actually, I do. Edward Oscar Heinrich. America's answer to Sherlock Holmes."

"Now I'm impressed." But Sean's smile faded. "And that's what I'm trying to tell you, Ab."

"Ab*bie*," she corrected, but it didn't even faze him.

"Heinrich was right about liars and cameras, Ab...Abbie. If you think of what you know about Charles and Olivia Cameron, you know you've only been presented the picture he wants you to see. He's a liar. I know it in my gut. In his hands, the camera is a dangerous instrument."

She put down her plate, too. He picked it up, looked to her to see if she intended to finish or not, then began happily wiping out what she'd left.

She'd never known anyone even remotely like him, or ever felt the kind of attraction she felt to him. He was so smart, so committed, so handsome, so aware of her one minute that *she* couldn't breathe, and so completely distracted the next that she wanted to scream.

He could talk her under the table about any conceivable subject at any given moment. He had more friends than she had acquaintances, so she knew he couldn't have sat around reading encyclopedias.

But everything that attracted her also made her want to escape him before she started acting like Lois Lane around Superman—who despite every other damned talent in the universe and the phone booth thing and the lantern-jawed good looks, always remained blithely, merrily, infuriatingly oblivious to Lois's feelings for him.

Sean Baldwin was cast in the exact same mold.

"Okay," she said at last, picking up the thread of his conversation. "Suppose we just bow out right now? Olivia got out. She's obviously capable, despite Cameron's characterization of her mental state. Why not just leave well enough alone?"

Grinning, smothering what in other cultures would be a compliment to the meal, Sean shook his head. "Well, there you have it, Abbie." His eyes were full of the devil. "My most blatant shortcoming."

She cocked her head sideways. "What's that?"

He looked up. His gaze traveled the length of her neck. Stuck on her lips. He sucked in a deep breath and cleared his throat. He reached across the space

between them and stroked her lips with his thumb. The
awkward gesture left her breathless.

"Fact is, Abbie Callahan," he said, "I have never
once been able to leave well enough alone."

SHE UNDERSTOOD without asking what his motives
were. It didn't matter whether Olivia Cameron had
pulled off a vanishing act to get away from her husband or her father. Someone was out to kill her. Sean
Baldwin might joke about never having left well
enough alone in his life, but he took his responsibilities seriously.

Olivia Cameron's life was at stake. Finding her was
a priority, whether he then revealed her whereabouts
to her husband or not. She'd agreed to help him.

They'd decided to let Charles Cameron go on believing his orders were the ones they would execute.

Abbie was there when Cameron himself grilled
Olivia's maid. What did she know? When did she
know it? Did she know who signed her paltry pay-
checks? If Jessica Sagermeyer knew anything, she kept
it to herself. Cameron told her to collect her things and
leave. He'd consider, when Olivia returned, whether
or not to bring Jessica back.

Abbie managed to hide her disappointment in the
way Cameron handled the woman. Cameron seemed
to intuit Abbie's disapproval—or else he felt that in his
zeal and impatience and fear for Olivia, that he had
gone overboard and regretted it.

"I...um, I shouldn't have come on so strong, but
damn it all, the woman must know something."

Abbie wasn't so sure. If Olivia had escaped, she
must have had help, and Sean was out even now
tracking down anyone with a clue as to whether she'd

managed an escape on the river. Abbie thought Olivia had almost certainly kept her lip zipped where the household staff was concerned. "Would you like me to talk to Jessica again before she leaves?"

Cameron halted his pacing. "Would you?"

"Of course. I'm not sure I'll be any more successful, but I will try if you like."

She found Jessica calmly folding clothes and packing shoes into paper bags. Her quarters were Spartan compared to the rest of the house, but comfortable. Abbie had lived in lesser places herself.

"I don't know anything," Jessica stated baldly.

"Maybe not about how Mrs. Cameron left—you knew the assumption now is that she left, and not that she was taken against her will."

"That's what I understood. But I've nothing to say to you."

"Jessica, please." Abbie sat on the stripped twin-size bed out of Jessica's way. "I came here because I thought I could help Olivia get past the rough spots, the public appearances. But I always worried that she would feel, I don't know, threatened, maybe, by my taking her place. Do you have a feeling that was true? Do you think Dr. Cameron was wrong to bring me here?"

"I've got no opinions." She scraped a hank of hair off her broad pale forehead. "What I do have, I keep to myself."

Abbie gave a half smile and nodded. "My mother was like that. She was a bookkeeper. I think she knew far more about the accounts than the CPAs who combed through everything she'd done all year every January. My dad had a lot of opinions, but then, most beat cops do."

Jessica glanced sharply at Abbie. "I am supposed to trust you more because you come from a background more like mine than hers?" Jessica's head angled up and in the direction of Olivia's suite.

Abbie's heart sped a little. Was it too much to assume there was something to be revealed to someone Jessica trusted? She shook her head. "Just...idle conversation."

Jessica ignored her.

"Are you afraid for Olivia?"

She folded a threadbare navy cardigan into her suitcase. "Why would you ask that?"

"Because I am. I'm afraid because she's slipped her bodyguards. I'm afraid she's been too insulated from the real world to know how to cope out there alone. I would be afraid if I were her."

"You're not," Jessica stated simply.

Abbie tried another tack. "Do you remember when Baldwin came to my room? You'd been downstairs, retrieving Olivia's ballgown. The circuit breakers aren't far from where you had to go." Jessica's hands stopped moving. "Did you see anyone? Anyone at all?"

"Only security." She flipped shut the suitcase. "Look. I've already been questioned until I'm so tired I can't see straight. I went to get the dress, I passed one of the security men in the hallway in the basement, I brought the dress back, I helped you into it so far as the skirt, and then Baldwin let himself in like he owned the place. That's what I remember, that's all I remember." She zipped her bag and hefted it off the bed. "If Mrs. Cameron had plans to leave, she didn't share them with me. I did what I was told to do, when I was told to do it, and this firing is the thanks I get."

"Jessica, I'm sure Dr. Cameron is just over-wrought right now. When Mrs. Cameron comes back—"

"Fat chance. She'll have nothing to do with what's gone before." Abbie didn't know if the maid meant Olivia would never return, or that when she did, she would not want to be surrounded by household help buzzing about her bizarre behavior. "You go tell Dr. Cameron," Jessica commanded, "that I had nothing more to say to you than I did to him—and my son is an attorney. If I don't see my severance in the mail, in a week, he'll find his candy-ass dragged right straight into court."

Her cranky voice rang with a finality Abbie could barely penetrate. She had to try. "Jessica, one more thing—"

"No."

"Please. Just this." The maid dropped her bag and turned back. Abbie shot her a grateful look. "We've assumed Mrs. Cameron left from the lanai off her bedroom, but when I went to tell her about the charity ball, her other door was unlocked, as well. I just opened the door and went in when I couldn't even hear Sachi whining."

"Are you coming to a question?" Jessica demanded.

"Yes. I thought Mrs. Cameron's door was always locked, that it was like a ritual she went through every night without fail so she could sleep. Do you know why it wasn't locked that night?"

Jessica had already said more than she'd intended, and Abbie had the feeling the maid had been about to laugh over the part about locking the doors so Olivia could sleep. But her answer, to Abbie's mind, was just one last snide remark.

"What did it matter? She wasn't going to be there."

FROM THE MOMENT Sean touched his thumb to Abbie Callahan's lips—why the hell he'd made such an intimate gesture in the first place he didn't even want to consider—his day went downhill. So did the next day.

The phone records he wanted were going to take at least one more day to produce. Some computer archive retrieval problem, no help for it but to await the repairs to the system.

The police reports on the murder of Peter Simons were missing, checked out to some detective who swore on a stack of bibles that he'd turned them over to the D.A.'s investigators weeks ago. Sean had no reason to disbelieve the detective, but the fact remained, the file was missing.

And along the river, for six miles in either direction, not one property owner, not one caretaker, not one security guard had seen or heard anything out of the ordinary between the hours of 7:00 p.m. and 2:00 a.m. the night of the charity ball, the only hours in which Olivia had to disappear.

If she'd had the cooperation of the whole of metro and suburban D.C. in pulling off her vanishing act, she could have done no better than this.

Sitting in the living room, which had been turned into a command central of sorts, Sean was not in a good mood. Cameron was making noises about calling in a team of private dicks to track down his wife, but if Ambassador Simons was right, when Cameron found her, she would either be returned here, to what amounted to a prison in her mind, or she would be dead.

Sean had Abbie's opinion to consider. Why, he didn't know. He was never averse to listening to someone else's opinion, but Abbie's somehow actually mattered, actually played into his own thinking. He had a sense that her intuition was superior even to his own. She still defended Cameron's viewpoint more often than not, but her grasp of the big picture sometimes staggered him. Her take on the ambassador and his agenda was one of those.

But if he had to choose between liars, he'd choose the ambassador. The old man might well be over the edge with grief or remorse or guilt. Abbie made the case that he could as easily have overstated the case against Cameron as Cameron had overstated his wife's inability to take any action in her own best interests.

But there had been no ransom demand, no call, no contact, no corpse found. Simply put, no reason to believe anything had happened other than that Olivia Simons Cameron had walked out on what had become an intolerable situation for her.

Abbie had to admit it was possible the relationship she thought she saw and envied so much was a sham. That the eminent psychiatrist Dr. Charles Cameron the world saw and so admired was not necessarily the man Olivia lived with. Public lies, private hell. Olivia exited, stage left.

Abbie had been on the phone, with the help of Olivia's social secretary, Enid Schomp, for most of the last two days. Under the guise of thanking Olivia's friends for their support of the charity ball, she found no one betraying themselves as having assisted Olivia's getaway.

Watching her hour after hour, on other phone lines himself, Sean knew he was in trouble—deep trouble. He knew the shape of Abbie Callahan's breasts beneath the mohair sweater she wore better than he knew his middle name.

His concentration wasn't off, only fractured.

His libido wasn't leading, it was charging. He admired her performance under fire with Olivia's closest friends, he admired her thinking, he admired how fast she was on her feet to react and speak her mind, he was awed by her logic, he even loved her when she was wrong because he was happy to demonstrate how wrong.

He'd made her spitting mad, twice, proving her wrong about meaningless details of Olivia's escape, but he knew damned well he was provoking her so he wouldn't have to deal with wanting to touch her so bad he ached.

God, he ached. And then he had to wonder if he was the one who was wrong about Charles Cameron, because every time Cameron was in the room, he let Sean know by some insipid, nasty little look that he knew all about how much Sean wanted Abbie Callahan.

Sean disliked the man intensely. He just wasn't sure why, whether it had to do with the lies, or whether it had to do with Cameron seeing straight through him.

But now, sitting with his feet up on the coffee table, Sean hit pay dirt. One call after another confirmed one more telling little detail. Maybe sensing his excitement, Abbie looked over at him.

"What is it?"

"Kenny Rorabaugh," he answered. "No one, not Delia Barry, not anyone at Protection Services, Inc., not any of his known associates know where Rorabaugh is. Or where he's been in the last ten days, for that matter."

"I don't...who is Kenny Rorabaugh?"

The prim and proper, ever-efficient Enid Schomp answered. "Mr. Rorabaugh was Olivia's bodyguard before Mitch Tensley. Dr. Cameron fired him."

In one of those dazzling leaps of intuition that made him covet her, Abbie guessed the reason. "Was there something going on between Olivia and Rorabaugh? Something improper?"

"Something, at least," Enid suggested, "of which Dr. Cameron did not approve."

"But it wasn't a romantic liaison?"

Liaison. The word hummed through Sean's lean, mean sensibilities like a laser, conjuring up thoughts. But he resented even thinking like that, not to mention the feeling. He stared at Abbie.

"No," Enid answered flatly. "Not that Mr. Rorabaugh would have refused Olivia had she any such thoughts. But I believe she thought of him more as a man she could turn to in the fashion she would have turned to her brother Peter had he still been alive."

"Do you think he would have helped her to escape?" Abbie asked, including them both in her question.

"There was certainly no love lost between Mr. Rorabaugh and Dr. Cameron," Enid said, "but he was otherwise such a straight arrow that it's difficult to imagine him doing such a thing."

"It isn't," Sean said darkly.

"Oh, Sean, it's such a cliché," Abbie protested.

"And a cliché is a cliché because it's inevitably true. Who else did Olivia have to turn to?"

She nodded. "It makes sense, especially if she missed Peter, missed having him to talk to."

"You're right on, it makes sense. The whole thing has 'professional' stamped all over it. Rorabaugh would have known the security system cold, he would have had time to figure the vulnerabilities, know how to thwart the hell out of it. He probably told Olivia exactly which circuit breaker to throw and when to do it."

Enid Schomp's hand shook. Abbie stood there looking at Sean, like he should have all the answers.

The problem was, he did. He'd gone to extraordinary lengths to prove it to Abbie, too. He didn't know Kenny Rorabaugh—it was unlikely enough that he'd known Mitch Tensley—but he'd seen it happen and heard the stories told a hundred times.

Men fell for the women they were hired to protect, fell for playing hero to her rescue-me fantasy. Far more often than not, when the gig was up and the money ran out, those were the guys who wound up bouncing drunks in seedy bars for a living. They'd not only made themselves unemployable among the rich and famous, they were cast off by the women faster than old shoes.

Sean had to suspect that, had it been Abbie Callahan under some big bad doctor's thumb, he might have found himself in Rorabaugh's position.

He knew there were huge differences. Important differences. Abbie wasn't coming on to him with that helpless, feminine save-me ploy. She wasn't the spoiled little rich girl in this scenario, either. Cameron didn't give a rap about her, and was, in fact, amused that

Sean couldn't keep his libido from leading him around by a nose ring where she was concerned.

There was nothing about what was happening between him and Abbie Callahan that was quite the same as a bodyguard having fallen for the woman in his protection. But it reminded him all the same of all the reasons he preferred to keep things simple with a woman.

Nose rings weren't his thing. He promised himself then and there that whatever it was about Abbie Callahan that had him tied in knots, must simply cease to exist, at least in his eyes.

The easier task, of course, which was the same thing as walking away from Abbie before she got any further under his skin, was to tell Charles Cameron where he could stick the little game of hide-and-seek he had going on with his wife.

Chapter Eight

For only the second time since she had met Sean Baldwin, Abbie felt real fear. Sean was truly angry, and it wasn't an experience she wanted for herself. He collared Cameron and dragged him off to his private study to remind him of places the sun doesn't shine, which was where he could stick this whole charade.

Charles Cameron sat at his desk, stunned to silence. "Hide-and-seek?" he croaked at last. "You think this is some sort of sick game of hide-and-seek? My God, man, it's only by the grace of God that she wasn't killed in that assault from the river—"

"I don't doubt that she's in danger. But maybe you're the one she's in danger from."

Cameron paled. "You can't be serious!"

Sean shrugged. "You're the one in control of the information. I've said it before, I'll say it again. You're a liar and you're desperate. The combination stinks."

Abbie watched Charles Cameron cave in on himself. She thought of Sean's metaphor in the forbidding little Thai restaurant, of Cameron presenting only the picture he wanted them to see. *The camera in the hands of a liar*... But she couldn't shake the intuition that the doctor was genuinely dismayed.

"Perhaps," he said, "you'll be good enough to explain to me where I've gone wrong, Mr. Baldwin, because my wife is missing, I'm terrified for her, and you're sitting there accusing me of being the bad guy."

Sean sat unmoved by Cameron's appeal. Abbie believed he would walk out on this assignment at any moment. She wasn't sure at all that she had anything more to contribute, either. But she also believed Cameron deserved an explanation.

"Sean? He has a right to answer your charges."

"All right." He turned to Cameron again. "Your father-in-law believes your wife was unhappy months before her brother was murdered." ·

"I explained that before."

"Explain it again," Sean commanded.

Cameron swallowed. "It's true we were having difficulties. I'd no idea she'd confided in her father, but after the miscarriage, Liv's hormones went berserk. Her behavior was out of kilter with any standards she'd ever—"

"How?" Abbie asked softly.

Cameron shifted in his chair. "She drove her Alfa Romeo through the garage door. She lashed out at our friends in public places. She...she wound up doing things, going places, disappearing for hours at a time."

"But you were working through it?" Abbie asked.

"Yes. I believed we were." He fell silent for too long, as if he'd forgotten what defense he was making.

"Then Peter was murdered," Abbie prodded.

He snapped out of his reverie. "Yes. Then Peter was murdered. Liv was inconsolable. There was nothing I could say or do." His voice cracked. "There was a phone threat made against her life. I hired a bodyguard. She put him through hell and back, as well."

Unconvinced by anything his employer had to say, Sean flicked at a piece of lint. "Who got the threatening call?"

"I did."

"But, of course, no one was ever able to trace the call."

Cameron shot him a venomous look. "You're suggesting there was no such call?"

Sean cut to the chase. "I'm telling you, sir, that the ambassador believes you are exploiting whatever comes your way to keep his daughter under your thumb. That you used her brother's murder for an excuse to fan the flames and keep her terrified that she's next."

"That's a lie," Cameron snarled.

"Is it?"

"Why would I hire a bodyguard except to protect her from real danger?"

"I can think of a couple of reasons. It feeds the illusion of constant danger. But maybe you just wanted to make absolutely certain she couldn't leave you. Why did you fire Rorabaugh?"

"This is absurd," Cameron railed, bolting angrily out of his chair. "I don't have to put up with this. I *refuse* to put up with these heinous assertions!"

The sun streamed through fifteen feet of multipaned windows behind Cameron. Abbie thought Sean had gone too far, but Cameron wasn't answering the question.

"Please, Dr. Cameron," she implored. "Can you just tell us why you fired her bodyguard?"

"Because he couldn't keep his peter in his pants," Cameron snapped, choking on hot, sick emotions. "Because Liv was horribly vulnerable and crazed with grief and that son of a bitch was taking advantage of her psychosis under my roof. *In my bed!*"

Sean bowed his head. Abbie thought the tumult of Cameron's powerful emotions struck even Sean's hardened heart. She felt sick, like throwing up. She wanted to get out of this house as fast as she could and never look back. Somehow she'd forgotten how to put her feet under her, get up and walk away.

However Cameron's emotional outburst had affected Sean, he went on. "Dr. Cameron, your wife is gone."

"Quite in command of the obvious," Cameron hissed, "aren't you, Baldwin?"

Unfazed, Sean went on. "You admit the most likely scenario is that she left under her own power. If you tell me you knew from the start that it had to be with Rorabaugh that she'd planned and pulled this off, then, fine. I'll believe you. I'll believe that she is still in real danger of the assassin who nailed her brother, the ambassador and Mitch Tensley. I will even take your word for your wife's fragile mental condition. But if you expect me to stick around under the handicap of half-truths and flat-out lies, think again."

Cameron collapsed back into his chair. "I just want her back, Baldwin. I just want to take care of her."

"She may not come back. Maybe she doesn't want to be taken care of by you."

Cameron swallowed hard. "I'm aware of that. But I can't stand by and let her recklessness—or Rorabaugh's—endanger her life. Someone wants her dead."

"Are you sure that wouldn't be you, Cameron?" Sean asked softly.

His upper lip twisted. "Her father told you that, didn't he? That I'd rather see Liv dead than with another man?"

"He believes that," Abbie said.

Cameron bowed his head. "He's wrong."

Sean waited until Cameron met his eyes. "Any particular reason we should believe you over him?"

"None," he conceded. "But with all due respect, Liv's father doesn't know how fragile her condition is."

"It wouldn't be that hard for him to put it together. It's pretty much a no-brainer, isn't it?" Sean asked quietly. "The ambassador is not unaware of the threats, of the constant fear—"

Cameron scowled. "Liv's father was not aware of Tensley's murder—or that he died bleeding all over her. She has been so fearful for her life she was suicidal. You must understand, Olivia had no base of security growing up. The vaunted, beloved Ambassador Simons found Liv and her brother Peter wanting in every regard. She became like a sieve. No matter how much love and regard I pour into her, it simply leaks away. She finds herself unworthy. I am not surprised . . ." His voice broke.

He couldn't go on. It didn't matter. The picture he painted was heartbreaking. Olivia Simons Cameron had taken her bodyguard to her bed to fill up a vast emptiness. Cameron felt the failure of his love for her to his marrow. Abbie felt his anguish to her core.

He sighed heavily and blotted his eyes with a handkerchief. His jaw quavered. "You would not argue that Rorabaugh is a suitable bodyguard at this point." He sat with his brows raised, waiting for Sean to agree Rorabaugh was not only dangerous, but morally corrupt, as well.

He had to settle for a nod. He straightened in his chair, then cleared his throat, putting his emotions aside. "Have you yet imagined the most dangerous outcome of Liv's actions?"

"I think I know what concerns you," Abbie said softly. Sean looked at her. Cameron turned to her, as well. "She may only have been using Kenny Rorabaugh to escape the estate."

Cameron gave a twisted smile. "You are truly quite intuitive, Miss Callahan. And if she succeeds...if she manages to escape him, as well, then she will be without even his measly protection."

Sean shook his head. "For a woman as emotionally crippled as your wife is supposed to be, your theories have her operating on a pretty functional level."

"To the contrary." Cameron looked at Sean as if he were incapable of reciting his ABCs, much less grasping the intricacies of a troubled soul. "How functional is such thinking, Baldwin, when the consequences are that she will leave herself with no protection at all?"

Abbie could see both points of view. If she had in fact run away with Kenny Rorabaugh, Olivia Cameron's actions were not those of a victim. She had taken steps to escape the threats against her life...but they were not the most rational steps.

"I would like very much to make sure she gets the help she needs. And I believe I deserve the chance to make things right for her. But this is all for naught if the assassin out there murders her first. You must find her. You must bring her back.''

His deep-seated anxiety preyed on Abbie's sensibilities like the subtle, edgy music in an old Hitchcock film. "Will you allow her to leave your marriage, or go home to her father, if that is her choice?"

He sighed and sat pulling his wedding band off and on, off and on. "I shall mind it very much," he went on at last, "if Liv chooses to leave me, but her life is more important than anything else. She must be found. I'm begging you. Find her."

SEAN WASN'T CONVINCED. Cameron had finally laid a few of his cards on the table, admitting to the ambassador's charges, confessing to having been jealous, even enraged by his wife taking Kenny Rorabaugh to her bed—to Cameron's own bed. He'd conceded to problems in the marriage. And if Olivia was just wacko enough to ditch even Rorabaugh, that was reason enough to find her, and fast.

But Cameron's lack of straightforwardness had already destroyed any faith Sean might have come up with. The ambassador believed Cameron was using them to find Olivia so he could punish her infidelities himself, but the point was moot, as Cameron himself had pointed out. Olivia needed protection, but if Sean and Abbie could find her, Cameron need not know until whoever was making the threats against her life had been caught. Or until she was physically and emotionally able to end it with Cameron—or return to him, whichever way it went.

It would have been easier, Sean thought, had he been able to make the case that if she'd run with

Rorabaugh's help, she was safe. That the man was a professional, and that in his care, nothing would happen to her. No assassin would get near. But the truth was, professional or not, by falling for her, having assisted her escape, having hit the road with her, Rorabaugh had sacrificed his objectivity. Without it Rorabaugh had also given up the necessary edge to adequately protect Olivia Cameron.

In short, Sean couldn't walk away. Cameron's wife could do with her life what she pleased, but only if she survived to make the choices.

Committed to remaining in the employ of Charles Cameron until Olivia was safe again, Sean knew he was also stuck with Abbie Callahan—and if he wasn't very, very careful, the same exposure as Rorabaugh. Sean's only defense was to treat her with the detachment of a friend.

It was going to cost him dearly, and he knew it. He wasn't used to fending off his attraction to a woman. He either acted on it with the clear understanding that he wasn't available for a long-term relationship, or he didn't.

He wasn't so sure he could do either with Abbie. He wanted her. He wanted to touch her, feel her white-blond hair catching on his jaw stubble, nuzzle her throat with his lips, taste her shoulders, tease her breasts. He wanted to guide her narrow hips and stroke her where it would drive her wild with wanting him.

He wanted to make love to her.

She appealed to him in so many ways he was running scared. He hadn't done any of those things, even touched her. At least, not more than to drag his thumb over her lips . . .

But there was the sticking point.

He didn't know the first thing about being in that kind of emotional space with a woman, and he doubted he could pull it off. He didn't want to find out he couldn't. Or to hurt Abbie Callahan by proving his certainty that he wasn't cut out for it at all.

So he told himself that what he couldn't afford was to allow what had happened between Olivia Cameron and Kenny Rorabaugh to happen between him and Abbie. That kind of involvement wouldn't fly. It would make him dangerously inept, off his center, out of the real game.

The decision made in his mind, he went off after her to map out a plan for finding Olivia. He found Abbie in the glassed-in gazebo on the north lawn.

The temperature outside was near freezing, but the day was as sunshiny and clear as it got anywhere near the river in November. Inside the gazebo, Abbie sat with Olivia's chic, lamb's wool, three-quarter-length coat around her shoulders, talking softly into a cellular phone.

She looked up as he walked in, but she was paying more attention to her call. "I understand your concerns, sir. I do. But we can't ignore the fact that someone shot at her. Someone killed her bodyguard." She listened again for a moment, but then held the phone away from her ear and closed up the phone.

Sean stripped out of his brown leather jacket. "The ambassador?"

She nodded.

"Did he hang up on you?"

"Yes." Abbie sighed. "He really wants us to leave this whole thing alone. He believes no matter what we do to protect her, Dr. Cameron will find a way to get to her—and it will be on our heads."

"You still don't believe it, do you?" Sean asked.

"That Dr. Cameron would ever endanger or harm his wife? No. I don't believe it."

"But you're sympathetic to the ambassador."

Abbie put the cell phone aside. "He's very old, Sean. He's her father. Of course he fears for her life. She's really all he has left in the world. I respect him, I admire him, I understand how anguished he must be, but I think he's wrong. I think we have to find her, and I told him so." She got up and leaned against one of the expansive windows, absorbing the heat of the sun. "So. What about checking on Kenny Rorabaugh? Where he lives, what he drives, when he—"

"I've already spoken to most of his known associates. Protection Services, Inc. His sister in Cambridge. His apartment super in Manhattan. No one has seen him in several weeks."

Abbie huddled tighter against the window. She wasn't used to this kind of cold. The sun-warmed glass warded off the chill. "Is that unusual for him?"

"Apparently. Delia Barry is unhappy about it. His sister says he's never been out of touch this long. She thought maybe he'd taken some job where he couldn't get in touch with her."

"Would he do that?"

"Doubtful. He has an exclusive contract. Lucrative, I'm sure. Protection Services pays well to keep its contract bodyguards in the stable."

"What did Delia have to say?"

Sean smirked. "In the first place, she was not happy that I even knew Rorabaugh's name. Once over that, she admitted Rorabaugh hasn't been out of touch or on a job assignment through the agency for more than a week at a time in five or six years."

Abbie drew a deep breath. "Sounds like he planned all along to stay available to Olivia."

Sean agreed. "But the smart thing to do would have been to tell Delia he was taking off for a while." He tilted his head. "If he'd been smart, though, he'd never have gone along with Olivia's scheme."

"Maybe it was his scheme."

"Maybe Olivia was just taking advantage of a guy who has the hots for her." Sean peered off into space. "He had the inside info he had to have to pull this off."

"Either way," Abbie said. "I guess it doesn't matter whose idea it was. But we're still really assuming that's what happened. Maybe it was someone we haven't even thought of who helped her."

Sean sat at last on the swing suspended from the ceiling. "We'll have more to go on when I get hold of the phone records. We know she had to have outside help, so she had to be talking to someone. My money's on Rorabaugh, though."

"Do you think she's safe with him?"

"From the assassin? Not for long. But if *we* don't know where they've gone, it's not likely whoever's waiting around to blow her away does, either."

Still cold despite the warmth of the heavy coat, Abbie rubbed at her arms. "This whole thing seems so unlikely to me, you know? There might have been political extremists willing to punish the ambassador in years gone by, but why now? Why Peter? Why Olivia?" She shook her head.

Sean stared out over the river. "Ab, you know, you have to look at who stands to gain. Who benefits the most."

"Who benefited from Peter's murder? Who will if Olivia is killed?"

"It *is* a no-brainer, Ab, if you go with the odds. Olivia inherited Peter's estate. Cameron will inherit Olivia's."

She looked pained to him. "I don't think that in this case the usual rules apply. Charles Cameron has everything a man could want. He doesn't need the Simons's family fortune."

Sean gave it up and backed off. Abbie Callahan was just incapable of seeing the possibility of evil intentions in Charles Cameron. He felt blindsided where she was concerned because he knew she wasn't naive and credulous. She knew evil existed. She was here to stand up against it. But she believed in Charles Cameron, and Sean was appalled. He wanted to shake her till her blinders fell off, but stronger than that, he wanted to shield her, to keep her, and her faith, safe.

He grinned, teasing her, lightening things up between them. "Maybe you're right."

Her pointed little chin went up. She was willing to be humored. "It could happen."

"It could," he granted solemnly. He worried that would be when hell froze over where Cameron was concerned.

"So, what's next?"

He knuckled his eyes. "Keep Olivia's lunch date with Candace Kemp. See what she knows."

According to Enid, Candace Kemp was Olivia's closest friend, and one of D.C.'s best-known socialites, a woman to whose parties congressmen and senators and every kind of political or social wannabe coveted an invitation.

Candace was the one person close to Olivia that Abbie had not spoken to, either the night of the ball, or in her calls in the last few days. Again, according to Enid, Candace had only returned from a trip to the Canary Islands the previous day. She knew that because the date of Candace's return to the States had meant she couldn't attend the ball—and dictated the timing of a luncheon date with Olivia.

"Candace is Olivia's closest friend. She won't be fooled by me, you know. Plus, Olivia would not have had a chance to confide to her whatever plans she'd made to run away on the night of the charity ball."

Sean nodded. Her reasoning inevitably impressed him. He had to ignore that, had to stay neutral, at least keep the level of his admiration for Abbie at a low simmer. "I agree. I don't think you should even try to impersonate Olivia with her. It won't matter. Kemp is a publicity monger, but she'll keep quiet about Olivia's disappearance."

Abbie frowned. "So what's the point in seeing Candace Kemp at all?"

"You never know, Ab. If nothing else, she may know how serious the rift was between Cameron and Olivia."

"I'm not so sure of that, either. I've had friends who went along for years acting for each other as if their marriages were just hunky-dory when the truth was, they were disasters. People—men—always think women tell each other everything, but that's not true."

"Do you seriously think it's pointless to see Candace Kemp?"

Abbie shook her head. "No. I just wouldn't hold out hope for any startling revelations." She left the window. "Ready?"

Sean took one serious deep breath. He wasn't, really. The more time he spent with Abbie, the less he wanted to keep his hands to himself, and the less interest he had in making her think he wasn't... interested. He'd just have to handle it. "Ready."

CHARLES CAMERON watched them depart the gazebo from the windows in his study. Panic filled his heart. No one had ever seen through his desperation as Baldwin had, nor ever called him on his lies.

He knew now how it was going to come to pass that he would lose everything. His beloved Olivia, whom he had cherished beyond reason or rationality, had betrayed him, not once, not twice, but three times now. He could no more assume that her love could be salvaged than he could hope to fly.

He felt himself closing in on certifiable dementia himself. Disoriented, sociopathic, schizo—he, the once neutral observer of other people's trauma, had been reduced to a beast, raging in pain, teetering on the edge of insanity.

The raging beast, which knew the betrayal, insisted that if he couldn't have Liv, then no man could. So Liv must die.

He all but choked on the poetic license—Liv, die, *Liv must die*—for the vestiges of his rational mind knew better. Liv must never die, or his soul would be condemned to hell for all eternity.

He laughed heartlessly at his own paradoxical

thinking, for it was all the *rage* now in the psychob-abble of chicken soup for the soul that one must fully embrace the paradoxes of life.

He didn't think Liv-must-die, Liv-must-live quite qualified. Had he been able to throttle her, insane with passion like Othello, he'd have long since done it. Or he could have killed her in some more calculated way. He might have set her morphine drip to a murderous rate after her miscarriage, or shot up her IV with a bolus of potassium to make her heart shudder itself to death.

He hadn't the stomach for it. The heart, yes, but not the stomach.

He just wanted her back.

And if by his clever lies he got her back, then what would he do? He laughed harshly again as if he could discount the tears welling up in his eyes. The infernal tears. He had danced to Liv's tune until he dropped. Time after time he got up and danced on. But to all the world, it looked as if it were Liv dancing to his music. What was there to do with a woman like Liv?

She would not be saved. He could not be her sav-ior. He faced the fact, but in the aftermath, he knew that he had emptied the vessel of his soul into her. Near the end, he had done what no rational being would have done, in the desperate attempt to assure himself that she would have nowhere to turn but to him.

His soul was certainly already consigned to hell. Maybe it was in that fiery hereafter that he was des-tined, finally, to have her.

His hands shaking now, he retrieved from the bot-tom drawer of his desk a box not unlike those protecting Olivia's diamonds and pearls, silver and gold. This box, however, contained mementos of his, and he regarded them with clashing emotions.

Madness, he thought. This is madness, when his practice swarmed with many women as beautiful as Liv, women who would fall at his feet for the favor of his attentions.

But it was Liv he wanted back. So the ambassador wished his daughter godspeed in her flight away from him?

Fingering the Army sharpshooter medals he had earned while his peers spilled their blood and spent their lives in the hellhole of Vietnam, Charles Cameron wished Abbie and Sean godspeed in pursuit of his philandering, beloved wife.

Chapter Nine

Sean, impassive as a chauffeur, drove to the exclusive high-rise penthouse Candace Kemp had obtained in one divorce and hung on to through two more. Abbie was just nervous enough about dealing with Candace that Sean's distant treatment barely registered.

She wasn't going to try fooling Candace in this one-on-one situation, but her failure with the ambassador still stung. And why Candace would have any reason to tell them anything at all was more than Abbie could rationalize. Still, if Candace could reveal anything of Olivia's state of mind, they'd be ahead of where they were now.

They had no trouble getting past security at the entrance to the high-rise private parking. Olivia's name, ID, make of car and license plate had to have been on a list cleared for entrance at any time.

They took the elevator to the penthouse suite. Candace's Puerto Rican maid answered the door with a welcoming smile. Candace, though, coming from somewhere deep in the luxury apartment, was clearly surprised by the visit. "Liv?"

Abbie swallowed and breathed deeply, handing Olivia's coat to the maid. Sean stood just to the right and behind her. "No, Ms. Kemp. My name is Abbie Callahan. I was hired as a double by Charles Cameron to meet Olivia's social engagements."

Candace frowned. There wasn't a wrinkle apparent in her expression, only skin pulled tight. She'd obviously undergone the knife or laser treatments of a highly skilled plastic surgeon. "I'm afraid I don't understand."

Sean stepped forward, offering his hand. "Sean Baldwin, Ms. Kemp. Olivia's bodyguard. You've been out of the States for quite a while?"

"Yes," she answered tentatively.

"Then you may not be aware that Olivia Cameron's latest bodyguard was killed."

Candace went stark white and sank into an exquisitely upholstered Queen Anne chair. "My God, no. Is Liv okay?"

Sean guided Abbie around the sofa. The two of them sat side by side. "She wasn't even injured," he answered. "But I wouldn't say her state of mind went unscathed. She's disappeared now."

"What do you mean, disappeared?" Candace demanded sharply. "Kidnapped?"

Abbie thought by her reaction there was no way Candace had known Olivia was going to bolt. Abbie shook her head. "We don't think so. There have been no ransom demands."

"What do you think, then?"

"That she ran away."

"Dear God." Candace took a deep, shaky breath. "I can't believe it. So much has happened to her, but I never thought it would come to this."

Sean leaned toward Candace. "A lot has happened. Were you aware that she had been unhappy in her marriage to Dr. Cameron in the last year?"

Candace gave him a cold stare. "I'm not sure that's relevant—or any of your business, frankly."

"Candace," Abbie said softly. "Anything you know, anything Olivia might have confided to you, might help us to understand. To find her. Did you ever have reason to think she wanted to leave Dr. Cameron? Was she afraid of him? Intimidated?"

"She might have been."

Abbie exchanged glances with Sean, and pressed on. "Her father believes Dr. Cameron was using her brother's murder to keep her in fear of her life and dependent on him."

Candace laughed unpleasantly. "Ambassador Simons could make a case against Mother Teresa."

"But why would he?" Abbie asked, liking Candace Kemp less with each brittle, caustic remark.

"Because he's a control freak. Because Liv was all he had left, and Charles took her away. It took him years to get her to even talk to him."

"It wasn't to Daddy that she ran, though," Sean said.

Candace scoffed. "That might take him another few years to get over. But it turns out he was right about Charles Cameron all along."

She met Abbie's eyes quite steadily. "If he chose to," she elaborated, "Charles Cameron could make you believe anything at all. There was no better strategy for holding on to her than playing on her fears that she would be murdered next."

Abbie looked at Sean. The woman's bald statement made her uneasy. "Are you saying Olivia was
going to leave Dr. Cameron?"

Candace wrapped her arms tightly over her abdo-
men and gazed out the floor-to-ceiling windows that
provided a spectacular view of the bay. She went on
only after a long struggle with herself. "What the hell.
You may as well know. Yes. Liv was on the verge of
leaving Charles months ago. Many months." Her chin
tilted. For the barest moment she made deliberate,
pointed eye contact with Abbie.

Stunned to her core with the look, Abbie groped for
anything to say. "What stopped her?"

Candace shrugged and looked away again. "She
almost died. Or... I don't know. I don't think she was
ever in any real danger of dying after the miscarriage,
but physically, she wasn't up to it. Then Peter was
killed. Charles Cameron was a saint all during that
time, but frankly, I think the ambassador is not far off
the mark."

She tilted her head again. The movement seemed to
characterize her, to suggest that what she was saying
had importance beyond the words themselves. She
reached for a cigarette from a gold-plated box on the
coffee table, and lit it, expelling the smoke in a rush.
"Charles has a way about him that gives me the
creeps."

Abbie didn't like Candace Kemp very well, and she
wanted to hear her bad-mouthing Charles Cameron
even less, but she'd demanded Sean keep an open
mind. She could hardly refuse to listen herself. "What
gives you the creeps?"

Candace's eyes squinted against her own cigarette
smoke as she studied Abbie. "One of his many fans,

are you?'' She tapped ashes into the crystal ashtray before her. ''No offense,'' she granted. ''I was, as well. It took me years to get over the hero worship.'' Her eyes narrowed even further. ''You see, I didn't get it until Liv began coming apart at the seams.''

Abbie felt herself growing cold again inside. ''I don't understand. How can you suggest Dr. Cameron is responsible for Olivia's unraveling like that? Her brother was murdered—''

''Ah, but Charles Cameron can build you up or tear you down with a look, and you won't even know what's just happened. He's truly frightening. When you could swear there is no way he could know what you're thinking, his...his way of dealing with you makes you think he knows anyway. Yes, Peter was murdered. But Charles undermined Liv's determination to get over it every step of the way.'' She gave a half-smile and dragged on her cigarette. ''You don't really believe a word I'm saying, do you?''

Abbie didn't. ''She was married to him for fifteen years. Surely if he had been as destructive to her as you're saying, she would have gotten out.''

''Liv was flattered by Charles's attentions for a very long time. Years. He knew without ever having to ask what she wanted, what she needed, what she dreamed of.'' Candace tucked a strand of her honey-blond hair behind her ear. ''She had it all. She had no reason to complain. It's very seductive, you know, for your lover to know you so well, to anticipate your every desire.''

She stared at her cigarette. ''But it all wore too thin, finally—or else the ambassador made her see the light of day. Whatever, when Liv wanted out, Charles began to see to it that she would never have the emotional stability or independence she had to have to make the break.'' She stubbed out her cigarette. "Is there anything else?"

Abbie felt somehow soiled, ready to leave, done with listening to Olivia's best friend describing how Charles Cameron could have perverted his extraordinary gifts. Everything she'd related had a ring of truth that made Abbie feel queasy.

It was one thing to be cherishing and alert and willing to make sacrifices and to have given Olivia everything, but it was quite another to be as cold-bloodedly efficient about it as Candace was suggesting. And worse, to be able to turn it all around to control her, to make sure she never left him . . .

Abbie had heard everything she wanted to hear. More than she wanted to know. "Only one thing. When was it that Olivia began . . . to want to leave Dr. Cameron?"

This time, Candace pointedly did not meet Abbie's eyes. "If I had to guess, I would say sometime late last spring, or early summer."

ABBIE KNEW there were more questions Sean would have liked answered by Candace Kemp, but to her it didn't matter at all. It was impossible for her to relate to a woman like Candace Kemp, but she couldn't accuse the lady of being prejudiced on either side. Candace hadn't spared either the ambassador or Charles Cameron in her scathing, brittle remarks. If she'd been one-sided about it, her charges would have been less than believable, but she hadn't. She'd nailed them both, and painted Charles Cameron as a real villain in Olivia's life.

Inside the car, buried in her own thoughts, Abbie just took a deep breath and accepted that she'd been wrong to assume that a brilliant mind and compassionate rhetoric made Charles Cameron a good man and wonderful husband. If anything, the opposite was true.

But none of that was nearly as important as what Candace Kemp had *not* said.

They were in the car, out of the parking lot and halfway to the Inner City day-care facility that had been next on Olivia's schedule for the day before Sean bounced the sedan into a back alley Abbie would never have turned into alone.

"Okay, Ab. I—"

"Ab*bie*," she corrected impulsively. "Abbie. Abbie. Two syllables, accent on the first. Try it."

He raised his brows at her.

"Do you realize what Candace was saying to us?" she asked.

"I think so. Charles Cameron is one twisted excuse for a human being and the ambassador isn't much better."

"Yes, but that's not it. I'm talking about when she said Olivia was prepared to leave Cameron months ago. And again last summer when things were coming to a head. Think about it, Sean. Think about when it was that she miscarried."

Sean switched mental gears and finally added up what Abbie had long since gotten. He looked sharply at her. "Cameron wasn't the father, was he?"

She swallowed and shook her head. "I'd bet on it, Sean. Olivia's relationship with Charles Cameron was done. Candace didn't have to stick a fork in it to know that."

"How?" He shook his head. "I don't get it."

"Well, you're a man."

"Yeah, and you told me women don't talk to each other."

"They don't."

"But these two obviously did."

"Maybe not." Abbie glared at him. "But, fine. Yes. That's what I said. If it will make you happy, say I was wrong—but I'm getting really tired of having to be wrong even when I'm right, Sean." She clamped her mouth shut, but not before recognizing that he was right again. He was wearing off on her. Now she couldn't leave well enough alone, either.

"You know what?" she demanded. "I think you're a twenty-four-carat fraud. You act like you don't even like me, but you do, Sean. And when that doesn't fly, you treat me like I'm some kind of *pal* of yours and you don't open doors for me and you just can't stand it when someone else is right, *especially a female*—really especially *me*—and I think if you had one teensy-weensy little bit of integrity, you'd just admit it and then you'd kiss me—and then—"

"Are you done?" he interrupted. He'd released his seat belt, turned in his seat, one arm slung over the back of it, one resting on the steering wheel. His eyes bored into her.

She swallowed. "No, not by half."

He blinked. "I think you've said more than enough."

"Well, there you go again. I'm wrong, you're right—"

He reached down and snapped open her seat belt. She had to duck to keep the strap from flying in her face, and when she did, he reached for her. His oversize hand closed around the placket of Olivia's lamb's wool coat and before she could register exactly what was happening or how he'd managed, she was in his lap, eye to Adam's apple with him. And a forbidden feeling, an excitement, a thrill, rippled through her.

Sean Baldwin was aroused.

She couldn't catch her breath, couldn't swallow, couldn't talk. Her eyes fixed on his lips. His warm breath touched her face and Abbie felt a pull of desire to be kissed by him so keen she ached. Her cheeks ached, and deep inside her, the ache moved in waves of pleasure.

He bent his head lower. Witlessly, so did she, to watch his lips, to see his tongue dampen them. To know when, despite the fact that he had already silenced her with his astonishing speed and strength and the power of his arousal, he would silence her with his lips.

Her world was there, reduced to the driver's seat shoved as far back as it would go, in his lap hidden by the heavily tinted windows of Olivia Cameron's car.

A sound came from his throat that sent the illicit thrill of it all spinning through her again, and then his lips touched hers and her world shrank even more, to his lips, to the breathtaking excitement of Sean Baldwin's lips on hers.

He groaned and shifted and took hold of her hair in his fist and slanted his lips to cover hers still more. It wasn't only his lips, but his arms around her, his strength engulfing her, his hand clutching her hair, his hard flesh beneath her—that made his kiss a moment of simple, deep sensual pleasure.

It took a rapping on the window, maybe a second or third, before either of them heard anything of the real world at all. As startled as Sean, Abbie looked behind her through the driver's door window. A cop was glaring at them both, jerking his thumb to indicate they'd better break it up and get out of the car or he'd take out the window.

"I don't believe this." Sean spat out a string of curses. It was only the second time she'd heard him swear, but she heartily agreed with every imprecation. He helped her back into her seat, which over the gearshift didn't go nearly as smoothly as it had going the other way. He cleared his throat, ran a hand through his hair, gave her a look that said, *What the hell, here we are a couple of thirty-somethings busted for necking in broad daylight,* then shoved his shirt-tail down his Levi's jeans with stabbing motions of his hand, opened his door and got out to face the music.

Abbie grabbed a brush out of her purse and flipped down the sun visor so she could see what she was doing in the mirror. Her body felt lethargic and startled, hormonal and scalding with embarrassment.

Jeez, Abbie, she railed at herself. There was hardly a hair out of place, and she couldn't have messed Sean's hair up in the space of a thirty-second kiss, but they'd both come up behaving like kids caught with their clothes half off.

She slapped the visor back into place and put her brush away. She was dying to hear what line Sean was taking with the cop, but she could only see him pulling out his wallet. A couple of seconds later Sean stood aside, the cop opened his door and told her to get out, too.

She swallowed hard and opened her door and faced both men over the top of the car.

"Officer Riske, ma'am. Let's see your ID, too."

"Of course." She couldn't even look at Sean. Fumbling through her purse, she came up with... Oh, God. Olivia's ID. She stared at it, not knowing what to do.

"Hand it over, lady," Riske commanded. She scooted it over the roof. "You folks old enough to take it to a motel?" He flipped open Olivia's wallet, looked at the photo, looked at Abbie and shook his head. "This you? Says here Olivia Simons Cameron?"

"Um . . . not exactly."

"That's what Baldwin, here, says. Says you are Olivia Cameron."

"Well, I was hired to be Olivia, but . . . my name is Abbie Callahan—"

"Ah, jeez, Ab!" Sean rolled his eyes at her. "Couldn't you just stick with the story?"

"If I knew what story you were telling," she snapped. "Besides, my daddy raised me to tell the police the truth." She looked back to Riske, who didn't look very entertained by this exchange. "Look," she appealed to him. "This is all a terrible mistake. We're very sorry, it won't happen again. My dad was a beat cop. I could tell you stories—"

"I'll just bet you could, ma'am," he interrupted tiredly. "Except the only one I want to hear is some real good reason why the two of you are gettin' it on in a car that don't belong to you in the middle of the freakin' day in a ghetto 'hood where the dudes'd rather cut your throat than look at you."

Sean had had it. "We weren't getting it on—"

"If I say you were getting it on," Riske interrupted, poking Sean in the chest, "then, buddy, you *were* getting it on."

Sean grabbed Riske's wrist on the last finger-jabbing. "Call it what you want, write up the ticket, write up ten tickets if you want, but do not jab at me with your finger again."

It wouldn't have been so bad if a gang of junior-high-age kids hadn't happened by just then, jeering Riske, cheering Sean. Riske's face went beet red. "Suppose you get back in the good doctor's car and you follow me. You don't, you'll get hauled in for public indecency, threatening an officer of the law, resisting arrest, and whatever the hell else I can come up with between now and five minutes from now when you take it up with my sergeant."

Sean was so irritated Abbie could feel the frustration rolling off him. "Look. This is just way out of hand. We were kissing. Is that a crime? I apologize, okay? Just let me pay whatever fine you want right now—"

"Too late, wise guy," Riske said, slamming his book shut. "You follow me, *now.*"

Sean watched Riske return to his squad car and banged his fist off the roof of Olivia's Infiniti. "Get in, Abbie."

She opened her door and slid into place, restoring her seat belt. Sean was already backing the sedan out of the alley.

"Can I just ask one question?" he said, falling in behind the cop car.

"If you could confine yourself to one," she retorted. "But I know what'll happen here. It won't matter how I answer, I'll be wrong, and you'll get bent out of shape trying to prove it—"

"Abbie." He looked over at her. She knew he was thinking about how buried they had to have been in that kiss for it to have taken Riske banging on the window with his billy club to get their attention. "Let's not get into what got us into this again. At least for a couple of hours."

"Fine. What's your question?"

"Sweetheart, what are you doing with Olivia's ID if you're not going to—"

"Don't even start with me about that, Sean. What do you think would have happened if I had said I was Olivia?"

"Well, since I'd just told him that's who you were, he'd have probably let it ride—and let us go with a warning."

"Wrong," Abbie said.

"Oh, you know."

"The same thing would've happened," she insisted. "He wouldn't have believed me."

"Yeah, Abbie, he would have. He had no reason to think you weren't Olivia."

"He already didn't believe me just looking at her driver's license! Suppose he wrote out a ticket and I had to sign it and he noticed that however in the Sam Hill I signed, it was not Olivia's signature. I haven't practiced that, you know."

"For cripe's sake, Ab, that's movie la-la-land B.S.! There's no way he was going to ticket you—"

"And there's no way he would have escalated to ordering us to his squad room if *you* hadn't decided to get wise with him."

Sean dragged in a deep breath. "Look, we'll get this taken care of in an hour or so, and then we'll just forget it. Deal?"

"Fine," she snapped.

"Fine."

But Abbie knew he knew, too, that there was no way either one of them was going to forget that kiss.

Chapter Ten

Riske was outclassed, he just didn't know it.

By the time Sean was done telling the sergeant which way the wind was blowing, the assistant mayor was on his way down to the station house, and Abbie and Sean, having never seen the inside of a holding cell, were escorted to a cushy conference room where the D.A. did whatever tap dances he had to do with whatever immune diplomats happened to have been wrongly apprehended. It didn't come up often, but when it did, the D.C. cops provided a very comfortable setting in which to assuage the overblown egos of foreign nationals for being hauled in on violations any ordinary citizen would have to endure.

Or something like that. Abbie put together the pieces from the terse conversation Sean had with Riske's superiors.

She sat silently trading glares with Sean while they sat in plush white leather chairs. The kiss to reinvent kisses was never far from her mind—or his, she suspected. When the assistant mayor walked in, they both got to their feet.

"Baldwin?" came this deep voice, struggling to keep from cracking up. "Sean Baldwin, Dean of the Goody Two Shoes School of Comportment?"

"Up yours, Dex." Sean turned and stuck out his hand. The assistant mayor, a bigger man than Sean, African-American, his head shaved for good measure, took Sean's hand and pulled him into a bear hug of a greeting.

"What's this going down, man? Public indecency? You?" Johnson gibed incredulously.

Sean shook his head and turned to introduce Abbie.

He looked closely at her, then looked again. "Sure looks like Olivia Cameron."

"Dex, my friend, this is Abbie Callahan."

He stared at her a little longer. "Honest to God, you could have fooled me."

"Yeah, well, you be a fool sometimes," Sean jived, but he shot her a look as if that proved his point that Riske would have believed her if she'd stuck with her story and said she was Olivia. "Dexter, here, is a jock. *Was* a jock. All-Pro running back three seasons in a row before he hung up his Redskins jersey for this monkey suit."

"Yeah, I'm respectable now, 'stead of one of those dime-a-dozen rich and famous jocks." He landed a punch on Sean's shoulder. "So. You gonna tell me what it is I'm down here about?"

Sean lowered his voice in some sort of stupid male ritual kinship thing. He jerked his head in her direction. "She was mouthing off, I pulled into an alley, we started kissing, and Riske busted us. Simple as that."

"Simple as that, huh?" Dexter plastered a too gullible look on his face.

"Yeah," Sean grated. "I suppose you've never pulled off the road to shut a woman's smart mouth."

"Won't deny it." Dexter grinned. "Can't say as I've had the need on me in a D.C. back alley in the middle of the day, though. You must have it *bad*."

Sean just shook his head, as if "bad" didn't quite cover the territory.

"Oh, stop it, both of you," Abbie cried, stamping her foot. She hadn't ever in all her thirty years stamped her foot, but these two yucking it up with their ridiculous macho, head-butting-caveman, locker-room, junior-high behavior made her really irritable. "This isn't very funny, you know! In fact, this is terrible!"

"She's new to you, huh?" Dex asked straight-faced. He turned to Abbie. "'Cause if you knew this guy, you'd think it was hilarious." He shot a gotcha look at Sean. "I personally have been waiting for your butt to get burned like this for what, fifteen years? Twenty?"

"Yeah, well, eat it up," Sean groused. "Paybacks are hell, you know."

"Yeah, I know." The humor went out of Dex's expression. "What were you two doin' anyway in a car belonging to Charles Cameron?"

Sean dragged a hand across the back of his neck. "It's complicated, Dex."

The former jock shed his suit coat. He had, Abbie was sure, as much power here as it was possible to have, representing the mayor himself. If she'd thought Sean was exaggerating about the scope of his friends, she knew better now.

"We're off the record," he said, tossing his coat on the back of the sofa.

"I was hired as her bodyguard. She's a double for Olivia Cameron. You know Peter Simons was her brother?"

Dex's eyes widened. "Holy cow. Yeah, now that you remind me."

Sean nodded. "Well, there have been death threats against Olivia, as well. One by phone that Cameron claims to have gotten, anyway."

"Didn't Mrs. Cameron's bodyguard get whacked in an assault from the river a couple of weeks ago?" Dex asked.

Sean gave him a sideways look. "I'm surprised you heard about it."

"The cops have kept it extremely low profile, true," Dex agreed, "but sooner or later everything filters through the mayor's office. Through *moi,* to be specific." He sat on the conference table, hunched, thinking, his arms folded over his chest. "I haven't heard there's been any resolution."

"There hasn't been. There were no eyewitnesses but Mrs. Cameron. The boat the hitman was using got away clean. The surveillance video is useless for identification purposes. So, no. There hasn't been any progress. But in the meantime, I was hired by Cameron to protect his wife—or her double."

Dex frowned. "You're the live bait, then?" he asked Abbie.

She gulped. "So to speak."

"I'm not sure I'm tracking this," Dex said. "You two were out...what, keeping up Mrs. Cameron's social obligations?"

"Yes. Today, and I went in her stead to the charity ball last Friday night."

"Raised a million three, I heard."

Abbie nodded. "It was very successful. But then the nasty twist is that Olivia arranged to disappear from the Cameron estate that night."

Dex's brows cocked up. "A planned venture?"

"That's the theory."

"Think the lady hired the hit from the river herself?"

Stunned by the assistant mayor's implication, Abbie looked at Sean, who was shaking his head. "I don't see it, Dex. Olivia Cameron is one hysterical woman on the surveillance video. Which doesn't, of course, rule out the idea."

"No, but then, there is no tie between whoever murdered Peter Simons and the death threats to Mrs. Cameron," Dex mused.

"Bright boy," Sean gibed.

"In your face, baldass," Dex groused.

"Yeah, all the time."

"Oh, puh-lease," Dex begged. "You don't even know 'in your face,' man! *In your face* is when the only son of a national treasure—otherwise known as the honorable Ambassador Avery Simons—is murdered. Next, I can see it coming, *in your face* is going to look like the ambassador's daughter turning up dead, too."

"No way, Dex. Not if I can help it." The two exchanged determined looks. Sean stood. "So, Mr. Assistant Mayor, can you walk us out of here?"

Dex cracked a smile. "I think that can happen. I can't speak for what happens next time."

Abbie started to assure Dexter Johnson there would be no next time at the same time Sean was saying the same thing.

Dex rolled his eyes. "Yeah, right. Anything else I can do for you lovebirds?"

Abbie blushed. Sean caught it. She wanted to do something really juvenile like make a face at him or stick out her tongue, but Sean had already turned back to Dex and landed his punch. "Matter of fact, yes, there is."

"Name it."

"Peter Simons's case file is missing."

"Now, how would you know that?" Dex asked in amazement.

"The detectives on the case say the D.A.'s investigators have it. The D.A.'s investigators say they logged it back."

Dex spun around. "Baldwin, you are too much. Always were—"

"Look. Dex. You may be my oldest friend, but you *ain't* my only. I asked for it, and it turned up missing. I need that file, and you just offered, and I figured if there's anyone around who can lay his hands on that file, you're the man."

Dex stood there a moment as if debating with himself, then went for his suit coat. "Wait here. I'll see what I can do." He swung out the door before Abbie realized she hadn't grasped what had just happened.

"Wait here?" she asked.

Sean shook his head in disbelief and grinned.

"What does that mean, wait here?"

His smile irritated her. He always knew everything. "It means, Ab, that the file we want is on his boss's desk."

"You're kidding."

"Makes sense," he argued. "In-your-face politics, just like Dex was saying."

"You think the D.A.'s investigators dumped the file in the mayor's lap?"

"No, I think the mayor pulled rank and took the file himself." He paused. "You know what?" He looked at her in a sweltering way he hadn't ever looked at her, not even when he was standing there watching while she'd tried to keep the mauve satin bodice of Olivia's gown in place.

"What?" she breathed.

"Ipso facto, Ab, if we hadn't been caught necking on a dangerous public thoroughfare, we would never have seen the file."

"Ab*bie*," she corrected for the gazillionth time, heat crawling up to the roots of her hair.

"Ab*bee*," he repeated dutifully. "Wonder what would happen if we were caught, say—"

"Don't," she pleaded, shushing him with a finger to his lips.

He took her hand from his lips and covered his heart with it, swallowing hard because there had never been a time he'd done anything so...rash. "Sorry, Ab. Never could leave well enough alone."

EXCEPT, Abbie thought caustically, that he was perfectly capable of leaving any well enough alone *alone* if he had something else to distract his attention. How could she fault him for not opening the car door for her when he already had his nose so far buried into photocopies of Peter Simons's file that he couldn't pause long enough to open the door for himself?

She walked around the car and took the keys from him and unlocked the car herself. "Get in the other side, Baldwin."

"Huh?" He looked up from his photocopies.

"I'll drive."

"Oh, yeah. Sure."

But she had to go around and open the passenger door for him when he stood there obliviously turning pages.

She had never met a more maddening man. The way he could kiss her, touch her, make her feel like the most exciting woman on the planet in a posh room reserved for delinquent diplomats ... and then go so completely off into another world, boggled her mind, to say nothing of her heart.

She shoved the key into the ignition, pulled out of the parking lot, and started driving.

He was infuriating, making her wrong when she was right, and right when she was wrong and all the while keeping her waiting with bated breath to be proven wrong again. And she didn't even want off the hook? She ... liked all this?

Abbie. Get off it, she told herself.

But then, she thought, following signs to the Beltway, casting herself into the third person like some tagline on a sitcom, Abbie Callahan's experience in the wide world of infuriating men was confined to a couple of lukewarm dates in college. And, in the last few years, to one or two nerdy souls who made tons of money producing movies from scripts she culled from slush piles five feet deep.

Abbie, she scolded herself again, taking the entrance ramp onto the Beltway. And the next ramp off. That wasn't true at all. She'd come really very close to marrying a visual arts professor from U.C.L.A. two years ago. He could recognize and create flash and razzle-dazzle and fireworks in his professional life, but he had zero for any of that on his own—or anything to laugh about, for that matter. Which was everything in a nutshell that made her crazy about—no, *over,* Sean Baldwin.

But it was the professor who had dumped her for a bimbette who wasn't even Abbie's natural blond.

Sean sat slouched with his knees propped up against the dashboard. He finally looked up from his photocopies and gave her a smart-alecky look. "Are you just waiting for me to notice you don't know where you're going?"

"I *do* know where I'm going. I just don't know how to get there."

"Mmm. Fine distinction. Where is it you're going?"

"Thanks to Officer Riske's overzealousness, I missed the afternoon with the Inner City day-care. There's nothing I can do about that. But I want to go back to Candace Kemp's place."

"You only had to go a few miles back downtown for that, Abbie."

"I know, but I didn't know which few miles."

"So you just thought you'd drive till—"

"You noticed."

"Isn't that what I asked in the first place?"

"Yeah, but you know what, Sean? You are so wrapped up in that file I bet you don't even remember what it was we were arguing about when we got into this mess in the first place."

"You mean, when we started kissing?"

"You know what I mean."

"Take a left at the light." He dropped his knees and sat up. "I remember. You were telling me Kemp was hinting that the relationship between Olivia and Cameron was over. So what's left to learn from her?

Whether it was even possible that the baby Olivia miscarried was Cameron's?"

"I already know the answer to that."

Sean scratched his head. "You do?"

"Yes. What's-her-name—the maid, Jessica—told me Olivia had been locking her door for a really long time."

"Which you take to mean, since before her miscarriage?" He frowned at her. "When were you going to share this little tidbit?"

"Just about the time you pulled into that alley to shut me up."

"Abbie," he protested, "you can't just go around keeping these things to yourself—"

"Yes, well, if you will shut up, I'll tell you my reason for going back to see Candace Kemp."

"Okay. You've got my attention."

"Good. If Cameron wasn't the father of the baby Olivia lost, then it might be important to know who was, don't you think?"

Sean cracked a broad smile at the obviousness of it all, but his pleasure faded as quickly. He put his knees up again and rested his arm on the window ledge and just stared out his window. "You know what scares the hell out of me, Ab?"

She knew what scared her. That despite his kisses, maybe all the more because of them, he would manage to consign "Ab" to the list with Dexter Johnson and the rest of his all-time great buddies. "What?"

"That you're not just another pretty face."

Which would have pleased her enormously—if only he hadn't looked so sad.

Chapter Eleven

Sean decided to let Abbie have her way; she would tackle Candace Kemp alone. He figured he could use the time off from dealing with her. He'd just walk out and sit on the pier that stretched into the bay and think about what he'd seen in the copies Dex had made for him. At least, that's what he told himself he was going to think about. What he really wanted was something to eat.

He figured Abbie would be safe from harm in Kemp's security building. He took the keys in case he was back early, but made her promise to wait for him in the building lounge if he took longer than she did.

He ducked into a bar long before he got out onto the pier, thinking he'd pick up a sandwich to go. But then he spotted one of his old Secret Service buddies hanging out in the corner by himself, watching an early Monday night football game.

Trace Freehling was his connection at the Washington *Post*—the one person he'd been unable to reach so far. Sean had hung around with Trace when they were both on Secret Service details guarding the lives of the junketing congressmen in the Far East. Trace had signed on with the *Post* when his tour was up. Sean just went to the private sector.

He didn't think it odd at all that he should run into Trace just when he needed him. Things like that happened to him all the time. He chalked it up to the many benefits of having friends just about everywhere.

Trace was drinking one of the house micro brews. Sean ordered a stiff Irish lager and a Reuben sandwich, which Trace claimed was unbeatable anywhere. They were shooting the breeze, catching up, Sean was piling fairly decent French fries away when Trace asked if he'd heard about Mitch Tensley.

"I heard." More small world stuff. He bit into his sandwich, chewed and washed it down with a swallow of his beer. "And I saw the hit in a surveillance video."

Trace's brows shot up. "How'd you do that?"

"I replaced him."

"Dumb and dumber. No offense, Sean, but why? You got a death wish?"

"Nah. I'm invincible."

"Oh, yeah. I forgot who I was talking to," Trace gibed. "Any chance of me getting some frames off that video?"

"To run in the *Post?*" Sean asked. "Dream on."

His journalist buddy nodded dejectedly. He might have been willing to strong-arm an acquaintance for a story, or a photo to create a story around, but he knew better than to try it with Sean. "This whole Simons-slash-Cameron thing is pretty weird."

Sean put down his sandwich. "What do you mean?"

"Well, everything that's newsworthy is killed at some level, except the socialite stuff. If Olivia Cameron hugs a homeless kid, that gets in. If her old man gets roughed up, that doesn't. If Olivia Cameron blows thirty grand for the gown for her charity ball—"

Sean choked. Abbie had looked pretty fine in that dress, but... "Thirty *grand?*"

"Yeah, in round numbers. So that's in print. But when her bodyguard gets blown to bits, that's not."

"I hear you, Trace. But the Simons family has been dropping like flies for a couple of generations. You can't blame them for throwing their weight around to keep that kind of crap out of the news. It's exactly the kind of thing that brings out all the nut cases, all the copycat threats, the—"

"Yeah, yeah, yeah. Security nightmare. You don't need to tell me."

"What else is weird?" Sean prodded.

Trace drained his glass of beer. "You know, there was a lot of stuff happening around town all in the same time frame that Peter Simons was murdered. I was following the investigation—which was going nowhere—"

"Except that the cops had concluded it was a professional hit?"

"Yeah—going on the lack of any other compelling evidence. FBI profilers say the particular caliber of bullet used usually signals a hired gun. A professional hit. So, anyway... the investigation was going nowhere. But the scandal surrounding Hal Gracie broke at the same time."

Sean asked for another glass of the beer when the waitress came. "Wasn't Gracie pretty high up in the justice department?"

Trace nodded. "You could say that. He was the one heading up the drug cartel strike force—which meant he was very high-profile, taking on the establishment, knocking heads together when the D.E.A. boys and Customs and the Bureau of Alcohol, Firearms and Tobacco got into their turf battles. I don't know how he ever got as high up as he did, considering he was a pretty outspoken proponent of legalizing pot."

Sean slathered more mustard on the second half of his Reuben. "I remember now. A lot of powerful people are offended by the mere idea."

"Right-wing ostriches, Gracie called them."

"And any one of those 'ostriches' would have gladly taken Gracie's head off and handed it back to him on a platter."

Trace grinned, but his humor faded. "He dealt with some pretty explosive issues. He had the press on his side because he was handling it all with a lot of cool. He was responsible for the bust in Arizona—sixty-seven million dollars in high-grade dope confiscated. Did you see my byline, 'Gracie Under Fire'?"

Sean grinned. "Sorry I missed that one, Trace."

He scowled. "Yeah, well it was a damn good piece. I think it would have gotten a Pulitzer nomination, except the next thing I knew, photos of Hal Gracie with some little dolly in a bikini turned up on the front page of the *Post*. Shades of Teddy Kennedy, only worse, because Gracie was such a law-and-order freak."

"Now that I remember." Probably because the photos hit every front page in the country. "But it turned out the photos were several months old, didn't it?"

"Yeah. He was still married then, though. Rumors started spreading that he was having an affair with someone else by then, although no one knew who it was. Anyway, the thing mushroomed until the president leaned on the attorney general, who leaned on Gracie, who resigned and skipped to Phoenix before she could fire him anyway."

"And this all has to do with the whole weird Simons-Cameron thing . . . how?"

"Well, hell's bells, Baldwin. If I knew of a connection, I really would have a Pulitzer with my name on it," he joked. "But seriously. Things go bump in the night, Sean. You know that. I know that."

"Mmm. Yeah. Things connect that have no obvious link."

"Exactly. Instinct kicks in and you know like you know your own face in the mirror that something is up."

"Yeah, well, what I see is myself getting set up."

Trace mugged a who-me look. "Blame my story-telling instinct." He proceeded to mangle Ray Bradbury's famous story theme. "A butterfly flaps its wings in the Bronx and a hurricane takes out south Florida. Go figure."

"I'm trying, bud, but you're not being what I would call exactly forthcoming. There had to be something that made the tumblers in your thick skull fall into place."

"Yeah?"

"Yeah. So what gives? Who's the missing link?"

"Call me crazy," Trace allowed. "But here it is." He took a fountain pen from his shirt pocket, stuck it between his teeth to remove the cap, then began connecting dots on a paper napkin.

THE CELLULAR PHONE in Olivia's purse rang twice. Once while Abbie was talking to Candace, the second time when she'd been waiting for Sean in the lounge for half an hour. Both times it stopped ringing before she could answer.

She could have killed him. He had the keys to the car, which was still in the secured parking garage, but he was nowhere to be seen. She wasn't even certain he knew the cell phone number, but if he didn't, that would be a first, and as far as Abbie was concerned, an unforgivable gap in his knowledge.

She thought it was him trying to reach her to let her know where he'd gone, but if it was, he hadn't given her one spare ring to pick up.

If he hadn't run into a friend, he'd probably made one, and in the meanwhile, forgotten completely about her waiting on him.

She was *going* to kill him.

She took the parking garage elevator back to the main floor entrance and went to the guard at the security desk.

He was maybe twenty-four, and even though she'd asked at least forty times if he'd seen anyone fitting Sean's description, he'd been sympathetic every time. Now he looked up from his paper. "Still no sign of him?"

Abbie didn't even need to answer. He knew. "Look. If you had an hour to kill in the area, where would you go?"

"That's tough. There have to be twenty places within a three block radius to go have a drink. The best food is out on the pier, right behind the building. The Harborview Bar and Grill, but it's not the best place for a woman to wander in alone."

"Thanks." The advice was probably sound, but the place was right up Sean's alley—a hole-in-the-wall dive with good food. "If anybody asks, that's where I've gone."

"Your call," he said, closing up his paper. "Take the elevator back down to the first floor parking, then the far exit. You'll come out maybe fifty yards from the Harborview."

It was already dark and freezing even in the parking structure. She shot a longing look at Olivia's car, then gritted her teeth and shoved through the exit door. She told herself it was too damn cold for anyone to be lurking around waiting to harass or mug her. She walked as fast as she could to the Harborview, then yanked open the door. A blast of smoky, stale hot air rushed at her.

It took her a few minutes to see through the blue haze of smoke and blazing neon lights strobing through the dark corners. But sure enough, there was Sean sitting on a barstool in the corner, drinking beer with some guy.

She would have sworn he saw her come in, but if he had, he'd looked right through her—or not even recognized her.

She should have called a cab on the spot and gone back to the Cameron estate without him, but the truth was, she didn't want to go back to the estate at all. Damn it all, she needed Sean, needed to share with him what she'd learned from Candace.

She hardly ever needed to tell anyone anything. Her friend Bibi would be amused—or outraged—at the signs and symptoms of Abbie Callahan in love.

But where was Sean when she needed him?

Huddled with one of his buddies, chewing the fat over a beer. She couldn't believe it. Railing at herself for caring at all, for being disappointed when she knew all along about Sean and his friends, she tossed back her hair and marched right up to the table, spotted the keys and grabbed them.

Which was when he finally noticed her at all. His friend was looking at her like he recognized Olivia— and she'd sprouted horns. Chagrin popped out all over Sean.

He stood. "Oh, God, Ab, I'm sorry! I just grabbed a bite here with Trace. Trace, this is Abbie Callahan, Abbie—" He broke off the introductions. "How long have you been waiting?"

"Oh, awhile," she snapped, bitterly angry with herself for feeling unnoticed and half abandoned. "The least you could have done, Sean, was keep ringing until I could answer the damn cell phone."

He looked confused. But then, he'd looked dazed enough just to see her standing there. "Abbie, I didn't call—"

"Never mind." She turned and stalked away, weaving a path through the haze and tables.

"Abbie, stop, will you?" he called after her.

"Not on your life." She didn't stop. He could sit there till dawn for all she cared. She was going to take the car, find a decent hotel room, get a room service bowl of soup and a salad, maybe a whole bottle of Zinfandel, spend the night, send for her things and decide tomorrow what to do.

Whether to dump what she knew in the laps of the police, or the ambassador, or maybe just lob it all back to Delia, was the decision. Either way, Abbie

Callahan was going back to California and leaving Mr. Obvious back there to deal with it all by himself.

She burst outside again. It looked against the light of the street lamps like crystals of ice hung suddenly in the frigid air, but she gulped in a deep, angry breath and turned to go. Her path was blocked by a couple of bruisers walking toward the bar, and they weren't making room.

She was just mad enough to slam their slimy hey-little-lady-come-have-a-drink proposition back at them, but she thought she'd probably burst into tears. It wasn't Sean's fault her daddy just hadn't come home one night, or ever again, and it certainly wasn't his doing that even when she knew she should get out of the relationship with the professor, she'd hung around till he dumped her.

But every time a man had mattered to her, he'd abandoned her, too. Sean was only the most recent. She clamped her lips tight and shoved past the idiot bruisers.

Sean came barreling out the door. She heard him shout at her. "Abbie, wait!"

She kept moving. She wasn't going to wait, but then she heard the two bruisers taking him on, hassling him about hassling her. She heard him warn them once to get out of his way. The biggest part of her wanted to leave him to his fate with those two, but she needn't have hoped he needed her even to distract one of them so he could finish the other one off.

The pair hadn't taken his warning, and the smaller one with the stained teeth and gruesome smile was already bellowing in pain and on the frozen pavement by the time she turned around.

Sean warned the second guy one more time, ducked a roundhouse swing, came up, hollered at her to wait again, then dropped the guy to his knees with some kind of deadly karate kick. The bruiser wasn't done, though. He heaved his two-hundred-plus pounds at Sean, and Sean dropped flat on his back in the blink of an eye.

She crushed the back of her hand to her lips to stifle her cry. Her eyes filled with tears for getting herself into this, for making Sean take on a couple of Neanderthals who thought they were protecting her. She couldn't decide whether to pitch herself back into the fray or run in the other direction. Before she could really think twice, Sean was back on his feet—and the bruiser wasn't.

Sean was wiping blood from his lip, though, and struggling to stand up straight. She thought she'd better just go unlock the car and be ready to speed away in case when he caught up with her, the Neanderthals had caught up with him. She gulped and turned and made for the garage. She'd just jerked open the door when he shouted at her again.

"Abbie, don't move! I didn't call—Abbie! Stay where you are!"

She remembered the exact tone of voice from the night of the charity ball when he had told her the one thing she'd better remember was to do what he told her to do, when he told her to do it, because otherwise she would get herself killed in spite of him.

She wanted to tell him to take a real heroic flying leap. Instead, she only turned and cried, pushing through the entrance to the garage, "I don't care if you called, Sean, just hurry it up!" She let the door go, hurried in the direction of the car, fumbling on the key ring for the button to deactivate the alarm. At least two other carloads of people were watching her from down the row of parked cars.

She had time to unlock the car door, get into the driver's seat and back out of the parking place before Sean burst through the door, screaming at her to get out of the car.

"Abbie, get out, *now!*"

Abbie froze. Her throat locked. In one split second she understood what the calls had been about, for the hitman to pinpoint her precise location, and exactly why Sean was screaming at her, running at her, diving headlong across the hood of the engine.

She was going to die in Olivia Cameron's car.

Shivering violently, inhumanly aware of every ticking millisecond, she pulled on the handle and threw herself against the door. Sean was there, hauling her out by the collar of her coat. He crushed her to his body, took them both down in a rolling motion toward the ground, and ended up on top of her, protecting her body with his own.

Olivia's car rolled silently backward, making the bystanders down the row shout furiously, but then it went up like a torch in a tight, hot, sophisticated implosion meant to incinerate its occupants beyond recognition. Flames consumed the inside of the car, every fiber of leather and wool, every atom of metal and oxygen, until the windows shattered, spewing white-hot glass in every direction.

Chapter Twelve

Even before the ugly twisting roar of the fire meeting fresh oxygen caught up with the blast, Sean stripped Olivia's purse from Abbie's shoulder. He flung it through a window into the flaming car, lifted Abbie to her feet and pulled her along behind him to the back exit.

They dashed through the door a split second before the building security team arrived to investigate. They might have been noticed but for the uproar among the bystanders. Sean pulled Abbie close, deep into the shadows of the parking garage when Trace Freehling ran up, spotted them, and became part of the shadows himself.

For a few seconds Abbie couldn't hear them, and the terror of not hearing was worse for her than the explosion and flying glass. But she forced herself to go still and focus, and in a moment, the low, urgent tones between the two men began to penetrate.

"Need all the help I can get, Trace," Sean was saying. "The car was wired, an impressive implosion, set on a delay to be certain she'd be torched in the fire."

Trace swore softly. "What can I do?"

"It will take a while for anyone to figure out there are no bodies inside the wreckage. You have to get to the cops, take it to the mayor's office if you have to. Just steer clear and let somebody else break the news. Olivia Cameron and her bodyguard just died back there."

"Done," Trace grunted. "You better scram." He held out his own keys and jerked his head in the direction of the pier. "It's a dark green '97 Jeep, parked down by the boathouse."

He banged his fist off Trace's, and then Abbie fell into step with Sean in shadows running all the way down to the dark, forbidding waters of the bay.

THEY HAD BEEN DRIVING inland in silence for a couple of hours when Sean exited the highway to gas up the Jeep. He pulled out a few bucks and told Abbie to go get them a couple of cups of coffee.

She saw for the first time under the gas station lights how terrible Sean looked. Her own clothes—Olivia's slacks and coat—were filthy, but the shoulder seam of his leather jacket was blown out and there were still shards of glass in his hair. His lip was split and the back of his neck was bloodied.

He started to get out. She put a hand on his arm. "Sean, wait."

He turned back. "We need to gas up and get back on the road, Abbie."

"No one's coming after us, for a while anyway." She stroked his hair, then brushed away the piece of glass that fell onto his shoulder. His jaw was darkened, either dirty or badly bruised. Her fingers touched him there and he didn't wince, but he looked like he'd been in a brawl anyway.

Her wrist lingered on his shoulder, her fingers at his jaw. "If you go in there looking this beat up, somebody's bound to remember us. I'll pay for the gas at the same time as the coffee, but I'll need more money."

He closed his eyes, indulging himself in Abbie's touch. He couldn't remember how to swallow. But he had to stay focused, now more than ever, which meant toughing it out, refusing her comfort.

Denying himself.

He peeled a twenty out of his money clip, slapped it down on the dash and got out without looking at her again.

Pumping gas, he watched her snatch up the bill, then go off, slamming her door behind her, to pay for the gas and bring back coffee. She was walking too slow, fighting the appearance of a limp.

His head hurt like hell and the rotator cuff in his shoulder felt like it was on fire. He'd meant to tick her off so she wouldn't touch him again, but he felt like a world-class fraud. Or worse.

He wanted her to touch him again.

Branding himself every kind of fool, he topped off the gas tank and got back into Trace's Jeep. Abbie took a couple of minutes longer. She got in without speaking to him, eyed him, then handed him a large cup of steaming hot coffee.

He couldn't keep his trap shut. "Abbie, I'm sorry. That was uncalled for."

"Well, you're a man."

"You keep saying that."

"You keep proving it." She looked at him. "Shouldn't we go now?"

"I want to know what you mean."

"I mean, you automatically assume that I have some designs on you all the time."

"Are you saying you don't?"

"I just wanted to see if you were hurt, Sean. I wasn't going to jump your bones."

He let out a frustrated breath. "There's more than that now, Abbie. Between us. A lot more."

She swallowed. "Why are we having this discussion, when you've gone to all the trouble of making it abundantly clear there isn't going to be any more?"

"Yeah, well..." His jaw clenched. If he had the brains God gave a goose, he'd have kept it that way. He plastered both hands around the cup. "I can't keep you safe, Abbie, if all I'm thinking about is how much I want you to touch me again."

She glanced sideways at him. He heard her swallow this time. Her eyes were wet, her lip caught between her teeth, and then she looked away and stared at her hands again. "You know what? Safe is highly overrated. You begin to know what's important when you've just been fire-bombed, or... or whatever that was. Could we just... for tonight, couldn't we just go to a hotel or something?"

He didn't know what to say, what to think, how to act. His head still hurt. His shoulder throbbed. A couple of hours down the road didn't begin to satisfy his protective instincts. But unless he was very, very wrong, and he was hardly ever wrong, Abbie Callahan wanted to spend the night making love with him more than she cared if she went on breathing.

He didn't want to be wrong. "Abbie—"

"Please don't say no."

He had never been so sweetly, guilelessly, hopefully propositioned in his life. Even when she kept her hands off him, she touched him where it mattered. If he thought he could chalk it up to wanting a one-night stand with her, he was wrong.

He was hardly ever wrong, but if it killed him, after what was left of the night, he would do what he had to do to keep her safe.

He popped the clutch, the engine caught and he drove down the road with his hand on her sore knee till he found a small inn, a decent enough place to take her that would also accept his cash without a bunch of questions.

Abbie clung to his hand while they walked in, and then to his arm while he signed Trace's name and got the room key. She'd never done anything so rash, or hoped for anything more. He walked her up the stairs and down the hall, then opened the door, lifted her into his arms and carried her through.

He put her down as if she might break, and stood there looking at her like he couldn't believe she was standing there waiting for him to make love to her.

She shed Olivia's coat. He stripped off his, then the holstered gun. Abbie stared at it for a moment, mesmerized. She had never been in such constant danger. His gun reminded her what the stakes were about. She might have died. She might never have come to this, with him. She began unbuttoning Olivia's silk blouse.

He wanted her so much he was thick with it.

She slipped out of the blouse, and then her bra, and though it was more unlikely than heaven on earth, he grew thicker with wanting her.

And once again, Abbie thought of Superman. For her this was better still than the magical moment in the honeymoon suite at Niagara Falls when Superman was finally free to be himself, to let go of his superhuman responsibilities, to give up being oblivious to the one woman in all the world who loved him.

Sean's transformation was like that. She knew the look of him when he was preoccupied, the skills he cultivated and lived by, the vacant expression he used to fade into the background, the inattentiveness he turned on her when he didn't want to be distracted from keeping her alive. But desire filled his eyes now. He hungered for her with a deep craving, a need so basic he became less than superhuman, too, and in his passion, more than any man.

She went to him and he touched her, filled his hands with her breasts. His fingers were magical, erotic and tender, greedy and indecent and sweet. His breath was hot on her shoulder, and when he lifted her and pressed her onto the bed, Abbie thought she'd just die with the pleasure of his weight on her and the feel of his lean, muscled back beneath her hands.

He stripped off his blue jeans, and they kissed. She slipped out of Olivia's slacks, and they kissed. She could have gone on all the rest of the night, sated by his lips and his tongue alone, the sensation, the heat, the pressure and depth and moisture. Drenched with her own need before he was half done touching her, she stopped him and held his face between her hands and asked him to come inside her.

"Abbie—"

She smiled. "Please, don't say no."

As if I could. He squeezed his eyes shut with keen, heated pleasure in her wantonness for him and her humor and her sweet flooding body. But when he answered her invitation and came inside her, he knew that never to be there inside her again would surely maim his soul.

ALL NIGHT LONG they made love. Once, a little after 3:00 a.m., Abbie got a washcloth and bathed his jaw and the blood from his scalp and neck, which led to a shower together, luxurious despite the ragged flowered shower curtain and puny water pressure. Again and again, afterward, they made love in the bed whose creaking springs made them laugh. But by dawn, Abbie lay in Sean's arms and cried.

He just held her. Reality intruded. There was nothing she could do to stop it. He thought her tears were a delayed reaction to the horrendous implosion of Olivia's car.

Abbie knew they had a good deal more to do with the sadness creeping into her heart, the certainty that his Responsibilities, capital R, would reclaim Sean. He would be forced to consign her again to his legions of friends.

She'd made her choice, her bold and rash proposition, with her eyes wide open. She could live out the rest of her life in bittersweet peace for one night such as this with him. She longed for a second, even a third, but she could only stand the rejection so many times.

So she would out-Superman Sean Baldwin and consign him to the status of a friend, a dear friend, first.

She got up to wash her face, dressed in Olivia's soiled clothes and tossed Sean's at him. "All that trouble to keep you out of sight of the gas station attendant... Wonder why neither one of us thought about the innkeeper remembering you looked like you'd been in a brawl?"

He gave her an odd look. "Are you okay?"

Abbie turned away. "Never been better. I don't know about you, but I'm starving. Think we can find an omelet worthy of the name?"

"Or something." He sat on the edge of the bed and pulled on his boxers, then his jeans. She made herself fuss over her hair, but it was an excuse to use the mirror to look at his lean, powerful body one more time.

Sean was already thinking about everything else. He sprawled back on the bed, picked up the phone from the nightstand and set it on his chest, then reversed the charges to call Trace Freehling. "Trace. What's going on there?"

He hung up within thirty seconds and related to Abbie the gist of the conversation while they left the room. "Things are in an uproar. The car bombing was all over the eleven o'clock news. The cops are being so tight-lipped they've refused to confirm anything more than that the car belonged to Olivia."

"Are they speculating that we're dead?"

"They're apparently not disputing that conclusion."

"Then we're safe, for a while? As long as whoever set the bomb believes we're dead?"

Sean gave her a skeptical look. The innkeeper greeted them at the bottom of the stairs, recommending his wife's eggs Benedict.

"I'm game."

Sean agreed easily and they were shown to the dining room, where there was only the scarred family dining room table and an antique sideboard. But they were alone.

"So, are we safe for a little while or not?"

"No assassin worth his salt is going to be happy until the deaths are confirmed, Abbie."

"I thought the point was that the bomb was going to incinerate us beyond recognition—or even forensic identification."

"It was high-tech. It would have reduced us to ashes. So what's a clever assassin gonna do?"

Abbie grimaced. "Wait and watch."

"You've got it, sweetheart. Whoever set the bomb was probably hanging around in one of the other cars—and knows damn well we got out."

"But he can't know where we are, or that we have Trace's Jeep—"

"He knows we're not dead, Ab."

She swallowed hard. "So okay. What do we do now?"

The innkeeper's soft-spoken wife pushed through swinging doors with their plates.

"Have breakfast," he said.

Abbie didn't think she had an appetite left, but Sean was already digging in. The Hollandaise was lemony tart and eggy. She gave it another try.

The oblivious look was back on Sean's face. Abbie sighed and slammed the door shut on her heart. "Tell me what you're thinking about."

He scooped up a forkful of coddled egg and English muffin. "Are you sure you want to get into this now?"

"We'd better."

"Abbie, there's nothing you'd better do. You can walk away from this anytime."

"I can't. Not now." She wiped her lips with her napkin, soothed to know she wasn't going to pop out into tears again. "Someone tried very hard to kill us last night."

Sean looked at her. "Who do you think that some-one was?"

"I... you're thinking Charles Cameron, aren't you?"

"Who else?" He cut into another bite. "Did you see the movie, *The Usual Suspects?*"

Abbie nodded. "I met the writer a couple of times. He's really an extraordinary talent."

"Do you remember the line about the devil? How his greatest trick was convincing the world he didn't exist?"

"Yes."

"That's Charles Cameron in a single stroke. He is the liar with the camera, Abbie, the devil who has tricked the world into believing he doesn't exist." He watched her while he washed down a bite with a gulp of coffee. "You still don't believe it, do you?"

"I believe he's gotten away with metaphoric mur-der, Sean—"

"But not the real thing?"

"No. He's extremely intelligent, I admit. Even..." She struggled for just the right word. "Diabolical?"

"I'd agree with that."

"He probably gets off on manipulating everyone and everything around him to his own satisfaction. He had the time to set up the car bombing, but to what purpose? We're no threat to him, Sean. At least, not enough to go to those lengths."

He put down his cup and leaned back to take Trace Freehling's hen-scratchings from his jean's pocket and spread it out for Abbie. He told her who Trace was, what he did, and how his favorite occupation was speculating with his spider web etchings over the conspiracies and hidden agendas of the Washington, D.C., power elite.

"This is why you left me stranded?"

He had the grace to look a little embarrassed. "It's pretty explosive stuff, Ab."

Her appetite was gone. She was tired of explosive stuff, real or on paper, but she put aside her plate and looked at the labeled dots Sean's friend had connected—the letters *CC* smack in the middle of a web with *PS, OSC* and *HG* at the outside, each of those interconnected, as well.

"I don't get it. This must be Cameron, Peter and Olivia, but—"

"The *HG* stands for Hal Gracie."

Abbie was stunned. "The justice department guy?"

"Yeah." Sean gave her a curious look. "You know where I'm going with this?"

"Maybe. When I went back to Candace Kemp, she hemmed and hawed around for half an hour, but when I told her I knew absolutely that Cameron was not the father, she gave me this funny look, and then she told me who the father was."

Sean gave a cynical half smile. "Hal Gracie."

"Exactly. But then she miscarried, and in the blink of an eye, the scandal over those photos erupted and sent Gracie looking for some hole to crawl into and pull in after himself. Didn't I read somewhere that he's living in Arizona?"

Sean nodded idly. "It can't have been an accident that those old photos of Gracie with another woman turned up at just that particular moment in time."

Abbie agreed. She followed the line Trace had drawn between Cameron and Gracie with her fingernail. "Does this mean your friend thought Cameron knew the father of Olivia's baby was Gracie?"

"No. It means Gracie was a patient of Cameron's."

"Oh, wow! One of Cameron's own patients was having an affair with his wife?"

"Enough to drive Cameron right over the brink, wouldn't you say?"

"But how did Cameron find out—or get hold of those pictures, for that matter?"

"You're assuming he's the one who sent the photos to the papers."

"Wasn't he? Who else?"

"In his justice department position, Gracie had a lot of natural born enemies—it could all be a freak coincidence."

Abbie knew Sean better. "You don't believe that."

"No. But Cameron wouldn't have had to look too far to find an enemy of Gracie's. Even then, when you factor in Peter Simons's murder—"

"How?"

"According to Trace, Peter probably knew Gracie wasn't Olivia's first fling."

"Wait a minute," Abbie said, stopping him. "This was common knowledge?"

Sean shook his head. "I don't think so, but Trace knows people who know people who knew Peter Simons was his sister's alibi for a lot of time they never spent together."

"So, Olivia was telling Charles she was with her brother when she was really—"

"Out cheating on him, yes."

It felt to Abbie as if she'd wandered into some impenetrable fog that Sean was seeing through without a problem. "This is too weird. What's the bottom line? Who killed Peter Simons?"

Sean got up to pour himself another cup of coffee from the sideboard. Abbie held out her cup, but Sean was in his preoccupied mode. It was so Sean of him not to think of filling her coffee cup.

Quick tears sprang to her eyes, which was when she got a glimmer of what it meant to love a man for his faults as much as his better qualities. She got up to fill her own cup while he spouted theories on the murder of Peter Simons.

"We have to go back to the old 'who benefited the most' question. At first, Trace thought Cameron may have done it—or rather, hired the hit on Peter while Cameron was in Paris at some international psychiatrists' conference."

"And he would have had his brother-in-law murdered because why?"

"Think of the timing, Ab. Peter was murdered shortly after Olivia miscarried. Maybe Cameron suspected that the baby wasn't his. So he turns to his brother-in-law, thinking he has an ally, only to finally get hit in the face with the fact that Peter had been helping Olivia keep her indiscretions secret for a very long time."

Abbie couldn't quite believe the twisted, tortuous motives. "But that isn't what Trace thinks now?"

"He doesn't know." Sean swirled the last of his coffee in its cup. "But he thinks it's even possible Gracie hired the hit because Peter was blackmailing him."

"Oh, this is rich," Abbie said doubtfully. "But let me try to work this one out. Say Olivia had been waiting twenty years to get pregnant and have a family, but it never happened with Cameron. She finally gets pregnant and starts seeing the filthy rich equivalent of white picket fences and swing sets, only Hal Gracie wants nothing to do with it. He's married. He's the voice of law and order and good old American values in the administration, and this will ruin him.''

Sean grinned lopsidedly. ''You do have a flair for this sort of thing.''

''Yeah,'' Abbie said, ''but get the stardust out of your eyes, Sean. This doesn't fly even in a Hollywood script. I can't see Peter Simons pressuring the 'power elite' Gracie to break up with his wife in order to marry his sister—especially since the inducement of the baby was gone once Olivia miscarried.'' Abbie paused.

Sean gave her a sharp look. ''What? What's going on in your head?''

Abbie shrugged. ''This is sort of what I do when I work on problematic scripts. Brainstorm a good reason *why*. Or how.''

''How what?''

''Well, for instance, I said I couldn't see Peter Simons pressuring Gracie. So if this were in a script, and it needed to be there, I'd have to figure out how I could believe Peter would do that.''

Sean leaned toward her, resting his forearms on the table. ''And?''

''And . . . I could buy it if I knew that Peter Simons believed, with all his heart and soul, that the only happiness his sister was ever going to find was with Hal Gracie.''

Sean shifted in his chair so he could stretch his long legs. ''That doesn't translate well into blackmail.''

''I agree,'' Abbie said. ''Once he knew Gracie wasn't interested, Peter Simons was smart enough to see that no shotgun wedding was going to finally make his sister happy."

"Once he knew, though, that Gracie refused to do the right thing by his sister, or that he'd used her and tossed her aside like some piece of garbage, Peter Simons was capable of striking back. That's Trace's theory, anyway. That Peter threatened Gracie with the photos. Gracie had to stop him. Gracie hires the hit, but Peter had already done what he threatened, and sent the photos to the media."

Abbie drew a deep breath. "None of this reflects very well on Olivia, does it?"

"To put it mildly," Sean agreed.

"We could have all this exactly backward," she said, thinking aloud again. "Isn't it possible that Hal Gracie and Olivia were truly in love? That they would do anything to be together? Think about it. Cameron would have even more reason to see him destroyed. Maybe Peter got in the middle of that, trying to protect Gracie from Cameron, and that's when he got murdered."

"Why wouldn't Cameron just murder Gracie, too, and shut off any possibility that he and Olivia could ever be together?"

"Maybe he knew making Gracie leave Washington in disgrace was a fate worse than death for him. I don't know." She exhaled and stared up at the antique molding at the ceiling. "I feel like every question just leads away from the real answer to all of this. We...or at least *I*, have been assuming up to now that the threat to Olivia was connected to Peter's murderer."

Sean tossed up his hands. "Cameron in charge of the camera, again, Abbie. Remember how he took such care to evoke the Kennedy myth? How Olivia turned twelve the day Oswald took out Jack, and graduated from high school the day Bobby Kennedy was murdered? Cameron very carefully framed the picture so that anyone looking closely would believe the Simons family was as ill-fated as the Kennedy's.''

"But he told us Olivia suffered from those fears from childhood."

"Maybe, or maybe that was one of Cameron's fabrications, too."

"No." Abbie shivered violently. "I don't think he was lying about that. Don't you see? The only way any of this makes sense is if Cameron deliberately set out to punish Olivia. She'd betrayed him, had an affair and gotten pregnant and miscarried a baby that wasn't his. Her lifelong fears gave him exactly what he needed to get her back under control."

"So you think he had Peter murdered to breathe a little reality into her nightmare?"

"Or else Peter got in the way of Cameron's retribution on Gracie. But even then, Cameron could have his cake and eat it, too."

Sean ran with it. "Gracie was humiliated, his career wiped out, he was practically ridden out of Washington on a rail—and Olivia was now living out her worst nightmare. Her brother was murdered, her father barely survived the attempt on his life—''

"By then, Olivia was already terrorized. Yes!"

Sean pulled his legs back underneath his chair and sat forward again. "It plays, Abbie, except for one thing."

"What?"

"If it was Cameron pulling all these strings, why would he bring us into the picture at all?"

"For the reason you gave me yesterday." Lord, it seemed ancient history now. "To feed the illusion that she would never be safe again. To keep her fears eating away at her. She asked him point-blank if I was to be her replacement."

"But then what purpose was served by setting up that car bomb last night?"

Abbie felt the blood drain from her head as a terrible explanation occurred to her. Her mind raced with the deadly possibilities. "What if Olivia didn't run away at all, Sean? What if he had it all set up to have her murdered while I was creating the lie that she was alive and well enough to go on with the Child Search charity ball?"

Sean played along some more. "Then all he had to do was get rid of us, and he was home free. For all intents and purposes, Olivia died in that fire, not on the night of the ball."

So agitated she couldn't sit any longer, Abbie rose and went to the picture window overlooking a small grove of very old spruce trees. "It was too late though, for that," she mused.

"Why?"

"Because the police will interview everyone in Candace's building. The doorman and the building security knew I was in her penthouse. She'll surely tell the police I was not Olivia. There's no way Cameron planned it like this—he's far too savvy to overlook a detail like that."

When the innkeeper's wife came to check on them, Sean stood, as well, paid her in cash for the meal, and told her they would be on their way in a couple of minutes. He went to stand near Abbie and began to gently massage her neck. "We're back to square one, aren't we, Ab? If Cameron didn't order that car bombing, who did?"

Chapter Thirteen

Sean had a few phone calls he needed to make, one to the friend who'd been trying to get the archived phone records in print, and the other to Delia Barry. One call or the other ought to confirm for them whether Olivia had escaped with Kenny Rorabaugh. If she hadn't, the only other possibility, and it was a remote one, was that she'd found some other way to get out, free of Charles Cameron, and back in the arms of Hal Gracie.

The third possibility, which was that Olivia had been dead and her body dumped in the bay the night of the charity ball, made all the other possibilities pale in comparison. But as they drove south toward Richmond, Virginia, Sean came out in favor of one of the first two.

Abbie wanted to know why, wanted a reason to believe she hadn't been party to a cover-up, for which Olivia Cameron had paid with her life.

"I don't think Cameron had the heart to kill her, Abbie. I think he was so sick in love with her—even after all the betrayals—that what he told us was the truth. He just wants her back, and he'll do whatever it takes to find her."

No solution to the problem answered why Olivia's car had been set to incinerate them though.

Sean drove through a pounding rain down the Virginia State Highway 29. Just outside Charlottesville they found a mall and purchased jeans and sweaters, a couple of coats, a duffel bag, and a few toiletries. At the intersection with Interstate 64, he turned south and headed back east toward Richmond. He could leave Trace's Jeep at the airport there, which would make it easy enough for his friend to hop a commuter flight and retrieve his vehicle.

Depending on the answers they got from the phone records and Sean's call to Delia Barry, they would figure out what to do next.

Sean pulled out his own VIP pass and got them a private waiting room inside the terminal from which to make the calls. Delia Barry was not in. Sean spoke to the receptionist at Protection Services, Inc. Lila knew only because Delia had been "righteously unhappy" that Kenny Rorabaugh still had not turned up anywhere, or called in.

The second call, to Sean's computer phone jockey friend, was even less productive. Hambone—the only name Abbie had heard—had tossed the files in a gym locker when he got the news of the car bombing, but he'd done a lot of work on them waiting for Sean to call back. Every number was cross-referenced against names. Kenny Rorabaugh appeared nowhere.

Sitting at the generic desk in the impersonal airport lounge, Sean swore softly under his breath. If he could have seen the phone records, he might have picked up on something that would still connect with Rorabaugh. "What about hotels, restaurants?"

"Well, there was one hotel on the list—several times…uh, the Sands, Standley, Star…something or other. Anything clicking here?"

"The Stanhope?"

"Yeah, that's the one. Does that help you?"

"Not really." The Stanhope was the location of the charity ball. Sean had called the hotel number from the Cameron estate half a dozen times himself. He thanked his cohort and hung up dejectedly.

Abbie wanted to wave at Sean and ask if he remembered she was there. His preoccupied mind maddened her all over again, especially since she had something relevant to point out. She cleared her throat instead. Loudly.

Sean finally came out of his fog. "What is it, Ab?"

"The Stanhope."

"What about it?"

She smiled. "You can be so dense sometimes. Sean, if you were Olivia, and making plans to get away, and you were counting on someone who had to be anonymous and reachable—*and,* if phone records were ever checked, seem just part of the background, where would you think to have Rorabaugh—"

He grinned. "The Stanhope. That's why I love you, sweetheart."

She swallowed hard. She wished he wouldn't say things like that. Not when, in the end, he didn't mean that he loved *her,* only something about her. "The problem is, we still have no idea where she ran to."

The phone at Sean's elbow rang, startling them both. Sean pushed the speakerphone button, but said nothing.

"You still there, secret agent man?"

He recognized the voice of his computer phone jockey friend. "One and the same."

"By the way, how'd you get out of that mess downtown last night?"

Sean frowned. "A story for another time, I'm afraid. You got automatic call-back or something?"

Hambone the computer jockey laughed. "I've got toys you wouldn't believe."

"Really, Bone?"

"I hear that tone, Baldwin, 'n' I get the feeling I'm about to be hit up again. Sorta like a sour stomach feeling, you know? Like when—"

"Bone," Sean interrupted. "Could you find out if any of the calls into the Stanhope from the Cameron estate went from the switchboard to a sleeping room?"

"Not a problem. Registered to this Rorabaugh character?"

"That's the one, but I wouldn't count on his having registered under his own name. Go for any room that wasn't being paid for by the Child Search finance committee."

"You're getting a touch more complicated here." Hambone was getting whiny.

"You can't do it?" Sean said.

"Yeah, I can do it. If I stay up all night playing with the damn thing."

"Yeah?" Sean gibed, winking at Abbie. "Well, take it one step further. See if you can trace any long-distance calls out of the one room you find, huh?"

They could hear computer keys clicking madly away on the other end. Sean scribbled, "Bone can't resist a challenge."

Hambone came back on. "Okay. Now listen up. Two things I thought of after we hung up before. One was, after about the twentieth or so of September, there was one less phone on the lines at the Cameron estate. That rarely happens, any less phones, I mean. Especially in a ritzy neighborhood like that one."

Sean exchanged looks with Abbie. "Did Olivia have a phone in her suite by the time you came?" he asked softly.

Abbie shook her head.

"Didn't catch that," the voice on the speaker-phone said.

"Forget it." Sean looked again at the phone. "You said there were two things?"

"Yeah. Other thing was, there were thirteen calls from the 602 area code."

Abbie looked at Sean. He answered her unasked question, scribbling the word Phoenix on a scratch pad.

"They stood out," he went on, "because each of them lasted for ten seconds or less before the connection was broken. All but one that went on for half an hour or so."

"Let me guess. That one came the day before there was one less phone on the line at the Cameron estate."

"Thought there might be a cause and effect in there somewhere. Chaos theory bores me stiff, you know? Random events colliding? Nah. You want—"

Affecting imminent snoring, Sean interrupted his friend. "Say good-night."

His computer buddy cackled. "Good night... Gracie."

Stunned, Sean and Abbie looked at each other and broke out laughing.

The phone rang yet again. Sean poked the speakerphone button one more time. His friend's voice came on the line, rattling off the information. "Eleven-six-one-three Escalante Boulevard, apartment number six, Phoenix, A.Z. Happy trails."

THEIR FLIGHT to Phoenix lasted a good five hours even though the time zone changes dictated three. If she hadn't already flown first-class on Charles Cameron's nickel to La Guardia, Abbie would have been too excited to sleep.

She zonked out roughly twelve minutes into the flight. But Sean had declared his 9 mm handgun and left it with the authorities, holster and all, to be transported in baggage to Phoenix.

He wore it so constantly that its absence inevitably left him edgy. He asked for a cup of decaf with cream and tried not to think about Abbie Callahan curled up next to him with her head on his shoulder.

He had never been so constantly on the verge of turned-on in his entire adult life. Abbie made him crazy. He knew she was pretending that they were just friends to avoid being hurt when he was acting like they were just friends.

He hadn't had his head on straight in days, at all. Dex Johnson had laughed his butt off, and rightfully so. If anyone had had the temerity to suggest that Sean would one day be nailed in a D.C. back alley, aroused and dazed and necking with a woman he was supposed to be protecting, he'd have laughed his butt off, too.

Then there was leaving her, *at all*, to her own devices with Candace Kemp. He'd flat forgotten her, and he knew too well it shouldn't have mattered how compelling Trace Freehling's insights were.

It was his own head doing its damnedest to blot Abbie Callahan from his heart that made him forget to go get her at the appointed time and place.

Then there were the hours spent making love with her. He'd violated just about every rule in the book, and he was lucky that Abbie was alive, *at all*. He didn't have a clue how to get her out of his head or his heart or his life.

The hell of it was, he didn't want to get a clue, either.

So he drank his coffee and asked for a couple of blankets. Pulling Abbie closer into his arms, he sank back and forgot to sweat it.

AT THE AIRPORT in Phoenix he produced the documents to reclaim his holstered gun, then ducked into a rest room to restore his weapon to its accustomed place. He rented a four-door sedan, bought a map, and handed Abbie the keys.

She gave him an incredulous look. "I've never been with a man who didn't seriously prefer to do the driving himself. What gives?"

He scowled. "Just drive," he said. There was no reason with the possible exception that he could watch her better if she was the one doing the driving. His masculinity wasn't all tied up in driving and he was about half ticked off that she thought it was.

At a quarter past ten the temperature had dropped to a balmy sixty-four degrees. Abbie rolled down the window to take in the warm, dry breeze as she followed his navigating.

"On the other side of this intersection—one more street to cross, no stoplights." When she'd gone that far he had her pull over across the street from 11613 Escalante Boulevard.

He peered through her at the building. "Six stories, from the look of it, all fairly spacious single units." The first, second and sixth floors had lights on, which meant Hal Gracie was either at home or careless with the electric bill.

Palm trees swayed gently. The clean, arid scent of the air reminded her of home. A couple of kids were whacking a hockey puck around a driveway at the next building over. Sean folded the map into its original shape.

"Have we got a plan?"

He forgot to answer her. He looked in a complete fog, but Abbie knew he was taking in every detail, and probably sorting through their options at the same time.

"Sean?"

"Yeah?"

"Do we have a plan for getting in to see him?"

"Let's see if there are buzzers, or if we can just walk right up to his door."

Sean released his seat belt and got out. Abbie followed suit. At this time of night the two-way traffic was light. They stood close to the rental car, waiting for a break from both sides, then crossed to Gracie's building.

The door in wasn't locked. Recessed fixtures lighted the foyer. Several succulents and cactus plants were scattered about. Abbie pushed the elevator button, and a small car opened.

From long habit, Sean held her back while he got on first. "So far, so good."

The elevator doors slid silently shut, then reopened on the sixth floor. In this foyer, leading only to Gracie's apartment, sand paintings and a couple of very colorful, primitive sombreros decorated the wall. Even to Abbie's unpracticed eye, the eight-by-ten-foot area contained no hiding place for fancy security measures like surveillance cameras.

Sean nodded to her, then stood against the wall by the door, out of range of the peephole, his right arm crossing his chest, his hand beneath his jacket, poised, Abbie thought, to draw his gun. Overkill, maybe, but they had no idea how Gracie would respond to a dead ringer for Olivia Cameron on his doorstep.

She drew a deep breath, pulled back her shoulders and rang the doorbell.

A woman opened the door. Several inches shorter than Abbie, a short-haired brunette, she radiated anger. It wasn't Hal Gracie responding to Olivia on the doorstep, but Gracie's wife, the one he'd cheated on so many times. "You've got a lot of nerve coming here. How did you find us?"

Sean stepped closer, putting his size twelve foot against the open door. "Mrs. Gracie?"

"Who are you?"

"Karen, isn't it?" Abbie asked softly. "I—"

The other woman peered more closely. "You're not—"

"No. I only look like Olivia Cameron. My name is Abbie Callahan, this is Sean Baldwin." She sent him an is-that-necessary look at his foot stuck against the door. "We would like to speak to your husband—"

Abbie broke off. Hal Gracie had appeared behind his wife. He was as tall as Sean, much smaller-boned, handsome, his dark brown hair graying at the temples. He stared hard at Abbie. "What's going on? Who are you?"

Sean subtly removed his hand from beneath his jacket. "Gracie?"

"Yeah."

Sean nodded, sizing up Olivia's former lover. "This may take a few minutes to explain. It is important. May we come in and talk to you?"

Tight-lipped, Karen Gracie looked up at her husband. He cast Abbie an indecipherable look, exchanged glances with his wife, then seemed to come to a decision. For whatever reason, he stepped back, pulling his wife with him. "Come in."

Karen Gracie led the way into the living room of the apartment. The local nightly news was on the television. She turned and sat without waiting, almost defiant in her look. Abbie wanted to reach out to her. She had gone a long ways with her husband, to the highest levels of the fickle Washington, D.C., society. To be living now in this apartment with its simple stucco walls, however comfortable, had to worsen her husband's fall from grace.

Sean sat next to Abbie on the sofa covered with a cheap southwestern design fabric. Gracie aimed his remote at the television to turn it off, then sat on the front edge of the rocking chair, tilting it forward. He rested his forearms on his legs. His hands hung loosely clasped between his knees.

"I presume this has something to do with Olivia. That's fine. I have no secrets from Karen. What do you want?"

Sean mirrored Gracie's posture. "Olivia has disappeared from the Cameron estate."

"What does that mean, disappeared?" Gracie asked.

"We think she ran away."

Gracie sighed, stared at the patterned oatmeal-colored Berber carpeting, then looked up again. "I'm not surprised. But if you hoped to find her here, you're wrong. She hasn't been in contact with me at all."

"Since when?"

"Since before she...went into the hospital last August."

"When she miscarried, you mean?" Sean pressed him.

"Yeah," Gracie snapped. "When she miscarried. What's your point?"

Sean met Gracie's trenchant look. "Your phone records."

The former justice department official sighed again and slumped back into the rocker. "Okay. I called her ten or twelve times. I wanted to find out if she was all right. I never got her, just the household staff."

"Until the nineteenth of September," Sean said.

Gracie knew then, what they knew. "Yeah." He turned to his wife Karen. "This was before you decided to take me back. I had no intention of ever seeing Olivia again. I told you that."

She nodded, but her jaw clamped shut against her emotional strain.

Gracie went on. "I finally got Olivia on the phone that night. We talked for a while. She was pretty upset."

"About what?" Sean asked.

"What do you think?" He darted a glance at his wife. "She was suicidal. She'd gambled and lost. She wanted out, she wanted to stick it to Cameron on the way out, and she wanted a kid. Instead, Cameron wound up more in control of her than ever. Other than that, I can't think of a single reason." His voice was thick with sarcasm.

"Her brother had been murdered by then, too," Karen said softly.

Abbie thought Gracie's wife was trying as hard as she could to find humane reasons for her husband to have called Olivia, rather than that he was still in love with her.

"Mr. Gracie," Abbie said, "it would help us to know what went on last summer—both when the scandal broke, and then when Peter Simons was murdered. You were a patient of Charles Cameron. Were you in love with Olivia?"

"I imagined that I was, but . . . I got a reality check when she turned up pregnant. I never wanted to play house with Liv. Karen and I have kids of our own, one in college, the other in medical school at Berkeley. I realized there was no way I wanted to start over with a baby. I just wanted what I wanted. The thrill of the illicit, maybe. Sex. Secrecy."

"What did Olivia want?"

Gracie snorted. "The same, she said."

"But that wasn't it?" Abbie asked.

Gracie shook his head. "Like I said, she wanted to stick it to Cameron—"

"And the clearest statement she could make was choosing one of his patients to have an affair with," Sean said.

"I prefer the term 'client.'" Gracie's lips twisted in an unpleasant grimace. He spoke without looking at his wife. "It was more than that. She set out to get pregnant. I wasn't her first affair, probably not even her tenth, but Cameron refused to believe Olivia could betray him. Getting pregnant was her answer. He could hardly ignore that."

"Are you saying Charles Cameron turned a blind eye to her affairs?" Abbie protested.

"According to her brother, it happened over and over again."

"You knew Peter Simons?" Sean asked.

Gracie grimaced again. "I knew him."

Sean focused hard on Olivia's former lover. "How did it all go down, Gracie? Was it Cameron who exposed your prior affair? Did he know the baby she miscarried was yours?"

Abbie knew Sean just wanted the bottom line, but Gracie couldn't seem to cut to the chase.

Maybe he didn't know.

After a few uncomfortably silent moments, he sighed heavily. "I trusted Charles Cameron. He'd come highly recommended, and I was under a great deal of strain. I, uh—" He flicked a glance at his wife. "I first went to him after Karen accidentally found out about the yachting incident with Amber Swanson. Cameron is the only one who could have orchestrated the smear campaign against me." He made an unpleasant noise, exhaling sharply through his nose, and swore. "Hell, I even told him whose yacht it was."

"Which is how he knew where to get hold of the photos of you with Amber?"

Gracie nodded, his expression resentful and bitter. "Three guesses how he got them, and the first two don't count."

Abbie felt sick. "The owner of the yacht was a . . . client of Cameron's, as well?"

"You got it. The guy never wanted to take those pictures. He reminded me how often things like that fall into the wrong hands. I just didn't listen. He was a professional photographer, so I knew he would develop them himself." Gracie shook his head. "I never even got prints of those photos. Karen was picking up our daughter from a party in Alexandria a couple of nights afterward and saw me with Amber."

"Your daughter saw you, Hal," Gracie's still-stricken wife reminded him. "I just called you on it later."

Her cold remark must have hit its mark. Gracie looked ashen.

"The point is," he went on, "Cameron had something devastating enough on my friend to turn the screws, so he coughed up the negatives, and photos I had never even seen went out on the wire services the next day."

Abbie didn't have the stomach to ask anything more. But Sean wasn't so similarly handicapped. "How did Cameron know it was you who had fathered Olivia's baby?"

"She told him," Karen Gracie snapped. "She didn't care what happened to Hal, or anyone but her—"

"That's not true, Karen," he interrupted sharply. "I'm not saying she wouldn't have told him. Hell, that was the point, wasn't it? That she was getting it on with one of his own clients? But Cameron knew before she was even coherent again after the surgery."

"Then it had to be her brother," Sean guessed.

"It was." Gracie scrubbed at his face with his hands. His eyes were bloodshot, his flesh still gray. "Peter knew his sister's marriage was this deadly little game of one-upmanship. He managed to keep out of it most of the time."

Abbie thought that must have played into the ambassador's hatred for Cameron. If Peter had confided in the old man, or even if he had only covered for her where her father was concerned, as well, the ambassador was canny enough to figure out what a sick relationship Olivia had with Cameron.

"Was there ever any bad blood between the two of you?" Sean asked.

"Never." Gracie steadily met Sean's eyes.

"Did he try to get between you and Cameron's wrath?"

"He might have," Gracie said. "I thought Peter could help. I thought he should take her back to her father's estate from the hospital, because if he didn't, Cameron would kill her."

Abbie wasn't following. "I'm sorry, but if you said how you knew Peter told Cameron you were the baby's father, I didn't hear it."

Gracie shrugged. "I heard they had a nasty confrontation at Peter's restaurant. I assumed that's what it was. If he tried to help her, he was in Cameron's way. Who else could it have been? Peter was the only one who knew besides Olivia. And me."

"Candace Kemp knew," Abbie said.

"Okay." Gracie frowned. Double lines like parentheses turned backward appeared above his patrician nose. "Include Candace then. It doesn't really matter how Cameron found out, does it? He did. Peter is dead, I might as well be. That's all the proof you really need. My career, everything I worked for and earned is gone. If Liv got out with her life, she's better off than either one of us."

Sean stood and held his hand out for Abbie. "Just one more thing, Gracie. Do you have any idea where she might have gone?"

"None." He got up, as well.

Karen Gracie sat where she was, but she didn't remain silent. Her dark eyes glittered with tears. "Would you tell them if you knew, Hal?"

He stuck his hands into the pockets of his cotton twill pants. His jaw went momentarily slack as he stared at his stockinged feet. He gave his wife a curt look. "I don't deserve that, Karen. You know it's over between Olivia and me."

But Karen Gracie clearly had not believed there would be any more affairs after Amber Swanson.

ABBIE WISHED with all her heart that she had never heard of Charles Cameron, or of his wife.

Cameron had lied to her from the very start, and she'd swallowed his lies hook, line and sinker. Where she thought she saw a powerful love, there was a terrible obsession. Where she believed there was a rare opportunity to stand up and be counted against evil, she had been used to perpetuate it instead.

Whatever else Charles Cameron might be, however brilliant his insight and books, he was a master of deceit and manipulation. Abbie was beginning to believe he had long since murdered his wife and sent them on a wild-goose chase looking for her simply to bolster the appearance of a man desperate to find his grief-crazed runaway wife.

Sean had to admit, driving through the lighted streets of Phoenix at a quarter past twelve, two days, now, before Thanksgiving, that Abbie could be right.

He'd been willing to shake her till her teeth rattled for believing as she had in Cameron's essential goodness, but Sean had wanted more to protect her from the ugliness. He'd been wrong—one of those rare times—thinking in the gazebo on the lawn of the Cameron estate, that Abbie was not naive.

She had been, and she was paying the price now. But he'd have given anything to spare her having to pay at all.

He took a light stab at easing her pain. "You could be right about this being a wild-goose chase, Abbie, but given your track record..."

He saw her swallowing tears. "I wish you wouldn't patronize me, Sean."

The passing streetlights glinted off her white-blond hair, creating a halo effect. He reached over to touch it, to stroke her hair. "I'm teasing you."

"I knew that."

"Then the idea is to quit angsting over this and tease back."

"Angsting is not a word."

He cast her an evil eye. "You know what I mean."

"Yeah. But I was tired of being wrong yesterday—make that two days ago. I want to be right, once, only it's just too hideous to want to be right about Cameron having already murdered Olivia."

"What you want, Abbie, is for there to be a happily-ever-after where the bad guys lose and the good guys win. In real life, things aren't that clear-cut. They just aren't.''

"I know that, too. But I believed Charles Cameron's lies. What does that say about me? Why did I believe him?"

"It's not a crime to take people at their word, Ab," he scolded gently. He stopped at a red light and flipped on the turn signal. "It's not even a character defect."

"No? What do you call it, then?"

"Inexperience."

"That's ridiculous. It's not like I haven't lived on the same planet with the Unabomber or David Koresh or Ted Bundy or those slugs who blew away the federal building in Oklahoma City. My father was a beat cop who died on the streets, Sean, so don't think I haven't been aware that evil exists."

The light turned green. He turned right, then left into the drive of a hotel. "There's a real difference, Abbie, between knowing evil exists, or even having it impact your life, and confronting it face-to-face. Do you sincerely believe if you'd ever seen any one of them walking down the street that you'd have recognized the evil?" He didn't wait for an answer. He pulled into a parking space and shut off the car. "Take my word for it. The answer is no. Neither would I, neither would anybody else."

"I'm not saying I should recognize evil walking down the street, Sean. My point is that I didn't recognize it when it was staring me in the face. You knew Cameron was playing games. You called him on it, remember?"

"Yeah, and I let him convince me to keep playing, too."

"That's not true, Sean. You were never playing his game. You never believed him. The one thing you couldn't ignore or walk away from was the threat to Olivia's life, and you knew all along that he was it."

Chapter Fourteen

Her voice trailed off until "he was it" was nothing more than a whisper, her throat laden with tears. His heart ached for her. He wanted to ask her what would have changed, what would have been different or better if she hadn't believed so much in Charles Cameron.

The answer, he knew, would be that it would have changed nothing. The trail littered with dead bodies, the course of events in the Cameron marriage, had been set in motion weeks before. Months. Years.

But he knew Abbie's reproach only had to do with whatever it was in her that made her believe in a liar like Charles Cameron, to let him exploit her.

Sean rested his head on the back of the seat. He'd been waiting a long time for her to come around to this. "It's a good thing to know, Abbie. Next time, you won't be the same woman who believed a liar."

He didn't know what else to say to her, how to make coping with it easier.

Her lips parted. Her eyes met his and locked in the dark of a parked car in the ritzy hotel lot. A far cry from the D.C. ghetto back alley.

A tension crackled between them. This wasn't easy; Abbie wasn't running, he wasn't going anywhere. If he'd been any different in all of this, he might have protected her better from the harsh realities of the big bad world at large.

He'd learned them early on. Very early, with an old man who knocked him around for the sport of it, and a mother too weak to get out or stop the violence. He looked for evil before he looked for the good, from long habit; one born before he was too old to choose it.

He hadn't been any different. His instinct was to protect her innocence, but the truth was, Abbie would be a stronger woman on the other side of this, no matter what happened. She would be stronger and wiser and more powerful because she would have left behind the part of her that was gullible and willing to believe the hype and excuses of a liar.

His mouth watered. He had to believe she could see the respect for her, the admiration in his eyes. That she understood this was no ordinary feeling for him. The tension between them edged up like heat lightning...gathering, building in the air.

He wanted to make love to her again. As Dex Johnson would say, the need was on him bad. Urgent as it felt, his desire for her carved deeper, loomed larger than the reason any male went full-tilt at a female of his species. He refused to explain it even to himself with the lame altruistic excuse of comforting her through difficult times.

He wanted her to know she was a woman unlike any he had ever known.

He'd been hard on his mother all his life because he could never figure out why she hadn't protected him when he was too little even to grasp why or how he got to be his dad's punching bag.

Abbie Callahan had the capacity to restore his faith and make him a better man, a more forgiving, less cynical soul. He just didn't know if he could live up to being the man she deserved.

The need was there between them. The darkened interior of the car was silent as a tomb, but he wanted her and she knew it. He was so aroused without even touching her that he ached with it. He didn't know if he could move. He didn't know what he was going to do.

"Sean."

Even her voice pitched his need. "Abbie, if you don't want—"

"I do." She swallowed. "You know better."

God, he hurt. "Think we can make it to a room without taking each other down?"

She laughed softly. He'd never heard a more sensual sound. "I don't know, Baldwin. Public indecency in two states in two days might be some kind of all-time record."

"D.C. isn't a state, girlfriend."

"You will never stop pointing out when I'm wrong, will you?"

"It's the reason why I go on living."

Her beautiful pointy-chinned face went all serious. "I don't think so, Sean."

"Why then?"

"Because you can't stop being who you are."

The respect and admiration deep in her eyes dismantled forever his notions of how his life was supposed to have gone on in her wake.

AT THREE-TWENTY in the morning, fresh from a shower but dead beat from making love half the night with Abbie, Sean slung a pillow against the headboard, tucked her head on his shoulder and placed a call to Virginia. Hambone picked up on the first ring.

"That you, Baldwin?"

"You know anybody else in the Phoenix area code?"

"Sure. I also know their phone numbers by heart. Let's see. You're in a Marriott—"

"I'm sufficiently impressed." More with Abbie's scent and the feel of her warm, still-damp body pressed to his side, but impressed with Hambone's fancy toys nevertheless. "Did you find Rorabaugh?"

"I confirmed a sleeping room at the Stanhope receiving calls from the Cameron estate. Problem is, there were no outgoing calls. Not local, not long-distance."

Sean flicked the phone away from his ear. This was not what he wanted to hear. He brought the receiver back into place. "Nothing then?"

"Did I *say* nothing?" Hambone railed. "Because nothing is not in my repertoire, you know. I think I'm insulted. I think I'm madder than a wet hen. I think you've got no sincere appreciation of—"

"Bone," Sean interrupted. He'd gotten really good, over the years, at heading off the computer jockey's discourses, but he wasn't in the mood for doing it now.

"Trust me. I only meant to reiterate what you just said. Nothing local, nothing long-distance."

"But you've never gone away empty-handed, now have you?"

"Never." Abbie's hand crept onto his chest. Her fingers threaded through his chest hairs. He closed his arm around her and trapped her hand.

"Well, bully. Thing is, you never know what you're going to find when you go cruising the domestic net, but there's always something out there. Your quarry is Olivia Cameron, right?"

"Right." He flattened Abbie's hand to his chest.

"Née Simons, still right?"

"Yeah."

"Well, you'll just never guess what her old man did last afternoon, long about 2:00 p.m. E.S.T."

Sean tensed. "What?"

"Well, I haven't cracked the investment accounts on Wall Street...yet. But I have my sources. The old boy must have cashed in a truckload of stocks and bonds. What he did next was to wire a couple of million to a numbered account in the Caymans and a little chunk of cash to an account at an itty-bitty bank in Wyoming."

Sean bolted upright and switched on the bedside lamp. "What's a little chunk, Bone?"

"Ten thousand. Pocket change."

Sean swore softly. "Is there a name on the account?"

"Turns out to be the bank president, but you haven't heard the interesting part. My source says the ambassador authorized wiring half a *million*. His banker apparently persuaded him not to do it. The federal bank examiners might get their panties in a real twist about that kind of changeover.''

Bone went off on a tangent again about that kind of money wired in out of nowhere suggesting payola or payoffs or earnest money on an imminent buyout. ''I don't know much about banking law, but you only have to look at all the fiascoes in the news in the last couple of years to see why it'd make the feds in certain quarters bite their finger—''

''Bone, I'm not tracking you. Does this have anything to do with anything at all?''

''Only as background for the real nail-biter.''

''Give it to me.''

''The banker was so concerned that he called his legal counsel, who paid a call on the ambassador. Said legal counsel returned with the unnerving suspicion that the money into the Caymans constituted one of three nasty things—blackmail, extortion or a kidnap ransom.'' Sean's jaw tightened. Another line had been ringing in the background of Bone's spiel. Ignoring it, his friend rushed on. ''That's it, my man. All of it. Gotta go. It'll be interesting to see if my sources clam up on this thing. Ring me later—''

''Bone, wait. What bank?''

''Oops. Guess that might come in handy. Wyoming State Bank, Saratoga. The last of the so-called independents.'' Sean let the receiver fall off his shoulder.

''What is it?'' Abbie asked.

''Get this. Ambassador Simons wired ten grand to a bank in Saratoga, Wyoming.''

''Oh, my gosh. Sean! Saratoga?''

Sean stared at her incredulously. "You've heard of the place? Other than the name of Peter Simons's—"

"Restaurant? Yes. When the ambassador and I were talking, he told me the name of this ranch where he used to take Olivia and Peter when they were children. The Rocking Eight, I think it was, somewhere outside of a town called Saratoga."

Sean rolled his eyes at her. "Abbie, for Pete's sake, why didn't you tell me?"

"Do you think Olivia's been there all along?"

"Abbie . . . it's possible."

She pulled the sheet higher over her breasts. "I'm sorry. I didn't mean to keep it from you." She paused. "I guess I didn't think it was even remotely possible that Charles Cameron wouldn't already have thought of it."

"He never mentioned Wyoming. It's possible he never knew of the place."

"She would never go there if he had. But wasn't it dangerous for the ambassador to wire money there?" The whole thing worried her. "Doesn't it just throw up a red flag as to where she's gone?"

Sean's brow furrowed. "Ten grand isn't an amount to get noticed by anyone."

"It's already been noticed!"

"By Hambone, sure. There aren't a handful of people in the country who've cracked into as many resources as he has. The other thing is, Simons wired the money to the bank president. Apparently another three million went to a numbered account in the Caymans. Olivia is either free . . . and set for life, or in worse straits than ever."

"What do you mean?"

"I don't know what came first, Abbie, the chicken or the egg, the Caymans account or the ten grand—but the ambassador tried to wire half a million."

"I'm confused."

"Look. If this is finally the ransom and the whole half million couldn't be wired, then it's possible the stakes went up, the kidnapper settled for the ten grand up front in exchange for the three million in a numbered, anonymous account."

"But this isn't a kidnapping . . . is it? She went willingly. She planned it all, right down to where she was going."

"It would be a nasty little twist in her plans, wouldn't it?" Sean got up and pulled on the last pair of new briefs from the mall package. "Think about this. We know she wanted out. We know she took Rorabaugh to bed right under Cameron's nose. So she convinced him to help her, she planned it all, maybe she even told her daddy every detail. But maybe Rorabaugh is no fool. He knows the odds are she's going to dump him. So he thinks to himself, *Such a deal*. Help her pull off the great escape, and then hold her for ransom. What's she going to do?"

"Oh, God." Abbie shivered, and found that she couldn't seem to stop. The chill inside just kept getting worse. Sean pulled on jeans, sat down with her on her side of the bed and cradled her in his arms until her trembling stopped. He kissed the top of her head, her temple, behind her ear, her nape. If he went much further he'd be back in the bed with her. "Abbie, you're dead tired . . ."

"I know. I do." She pulled away. "Mostly tired of trying to second-guess what's really happening, though." Sean got up. She pulled the blanket closer, but she knew there was really no way to dispel the kind of chill that came from deep-seated fear. "Tell me Rorabaugh wouldn't kill her."

"My guess is that he won't. But who really knows? If he's done this, she might want to kill him. In a contest, I'd have to pick Rorabaugh."

"I'm not so sure. I don't think Olivia can be pushed much further before she snaps." She fell silent for a moment. "Sean, this bank thing really bothers me. What about her own money? If she planned all this as carefully as it appears, wouldn't she have transferred money out of her own accounts?"

"Not if it would tip her hand to Cameron."

She nodded, seeing the logic. "She couldn't pay Rorabaugh off herself, then. So if he turned the tables on her, when it came to making the ransom demand, even Rorabaugh knew it was better to hit up her father than her husband."

"Except that it's Cameron who wants her back so desperately."

"For all we know, he's been hit up, too." She gave a cynical little laugh. "Shall we call him and ask?"

Sean looked at her as if she'd lost her mind.

"It was a joke." She watched him pull blue jeans on over his tight, lean thighs. She shivered. "Sean?"

"Yeah?"

"Do you really believe Olivia's escape has turned into a kidnapping? Maybe everything is still going according to her original plan. Maybe she was counting on her father to funnel money to her."

Sean gave a tired sigh. "I don't know, Abbie. Hambone's source said the banker's attorney paid a visit to Ambassador Simons, and came away with the impression that the old guy was meeting a ransom demand." Fighting with the tags on a new pullover sweater, he bit into the plastic string. "In my gut, I know there's something we're still not getting."

"Well, for one thing, Olivia's track record with men isn't what I would call smart."

She pushed aside the covers and began dressing. It may have been the middle of the night, but it was apparent Sean would be out the door in another few seconds. He wasn't going to get away with ditching her here. He'd made it pretty clear to her in the last few hours that Cameron's wild-goose chase wasn't worth her life.

She didn't want any arguments now. She wasn't going to ask where they were headed. She was just going to tag along, stuck to him like a burr.

He was agreeing with her assessment of Olivia's faulty taste in men. "Then look at it from Rorabaugh's perspective. He's out there risking his neck and busting his butt every day to protect these filthy rich crybabies. He won't earn in a lifetime what Olivia Cameron spends on clothes and jewelry every year. Put him into a situation where the clients are already playing deadly little games with each other, he decides he can play, too. I wouldn't put it past him to try to grab a scot-free three million dollars."

Abbie pulled on her socks and shoes. She felt edgy, restless, needing to take a walk or do a hard hour of yoga stretches. "I just want to know one thing."

He tossed the rest of both their things into the duffel bag. "What is it, Abbie?"

"If we go there, will we just make things worse? Shouldn't we notify the authorities?"

"That's two questions." He took her into his arms. "I hate to be the one to point this out, but two is always greater than one."

"Profound, Baldwin." Refusing to rise to the bait, or to consider whether he had meant any double entendre by his reply, she laid her head on his shoulder. "One answer will do."

He cradled her body close. "You sure I can't put you on a plane back to Los Angeles?"

"One answer," she said, inhaling his scent, memorizing the feel of his arms around her, "not another question."

"Things will heat up, Abbie. You can count on it."

SHE PROMISED HIM on their way back to the airport that if he told her to stay, duck, hit the ground, or run like hell, she would do it.

Her track record in that regard wasn't exactly sterling, either. If he couldn't count on her to do what he told her to do, when he told her to do it, just exactly as he had commanded days ago on their way to the Child Search ball, then she wasn't going at all. She got the message loud and clear. She would have walked on a bed of nails to be with him for another day.

For a lifetime, she might have sold her soul, but he wasn't asking. She was more than a friend in his mind, she knew that, but she didn't know what that meant. What was more than a friend and less than forever after?

A good friend.

A shadow lover, here and gone, stealing into her heart at all the wrong moments for the rest of her life. But she would have these hours with him to remember. She'd known better than to hope for any more from the very start.

She plucked her spirits up and reminded herself that there was nothing better in life than good friends. He held her hand all the way to the ticket counter and the one clerk serving customers in the middle of the night.

The closest thing to a flight anywhere near Saratoga, Wyoming, was one departing eight hours later, and that would only get them to Cheyenne. They'd have to rent a car and drive another two or three hours after that. Sean asked for the number of a private carrier.

The clerk searched through a drawerful of papers and finally came up with a list of three possibilities. With Sean's usual run of good timing and better luck, the first one connected. At a private hangar they met the pilot of a four-seater based in Colorado that brought big-time fly fishermen in and out of Saratoga by the handfuls all summer long.

His red hair had faded with age. His hands were spotted with freckles, and he must have weighed no more than a hundred and ten, dripping wet. But he knew the owners of what was loosely termed a resort, too, and though they didn't as a rule take guests in winter, for an additional sum, he'd get them a place to stay and a four-wheel drive to get around in. A paltry twenty-five hundred dollars in cash would cover the bill for three, maybe four days.

Which all supposed the weather was going to co-operate.

The pilot went off to check the flying conditions. Sean and Abbie drove back to the main terminal so he could hit up an ATM for thirty of the recently rede-signed one hundred dollar bills.

"Is there a whole lot more where that comes from?" Abbie asked, wide-eyed. Her cash card would be good for half that amount on a really flush day.

"Considering Cameron isn't likely to pay Protec-tion Services, Inc. for my services. I hate plastic." He rambled on. None of which really answered her ques-tion. He was, she noticed with a sigh, back into his oblivious mode.

He worried, she knew, that with the ambassador's ten grand wired yesterday to the bank in Saratoga, the game might have already played out. Olivia could be long since dead, or gone, depending on Rorabaugh.

The sun cracked over the eastern horizon as Sean sped back to the private plane hangar, debating mostly with himself over calling the bank to see if the money was still there. This whole thing had finally reached its lowest common denominator, which meant Sean had run out of friends he could tap. He couldn't think of a single person in his vast acquaintance who could vouch for him or anything he had to say to a Wyo-ming banker.

The ruddy pilot returned to the bare-bones waiting room with the information that I-80 had been closed between Cheyenne and Rock Springs—most of the way across Wyoming—for the past thirty-six hours. Everything south of the interstate to the Colorado border, which included Saratoga, had been socked in by a blizzard, as well. Guesstimates had it staying that way for a minimum six more hours.

The pilot saw no problem with that. Flying was not the problem, only a place to land. By his reckoning, leaving as soon as he could complete his checklists, they'd arrive about the same time a landing strip could be cleared.

Sean had no problems, either. He was cheered by the news, truth be told, because the blizzard meant no one could have ducked in or out of the area since the ambassador's money hit the bank yesterday.

Once on the plane, Abbie had the problems. The back seat where she was consigned was more cramped than the seats in Bibi's vintage VW Bug, the unexpected air pockets, or down drafts or whatever they were, made her stomach pitch and groan. She had to use the facilities and there were none. She couldn't hear half of what Sean said to her, never mind the pilot.

She would have given anything to just drift off, but the cold, cramped space and the constant white noise made sleeping a joke.

Sean turned a worried look on her a few minutes out of Saratoga. Something about the landing. About being flagged off the landing strip, and onto the highway.

The plane lost speed and altitude at a sickening rate. Abbie gritted her teeth and clamped her eyes shut and reconsidered what it meant to have a few more hours with Sean, but the landing came off perfectly. Taxiing along the snow-covered two-lane highway, the plane slowed, then stopped. Without shutting down the engine, the pilot maneuvered around inside to let them out. He would be back, but he had to get back to Denver.

Standing to the side of the road at a gray-and-burgundy Ford Bronco, a nattily dressed man awaited them. Automatically wary, Sean shoved Abbie behind him as the other man advanced toward them.

He wore dark glasses and an expensive, full-length sheepskin coat over a business suit. The chunk of silver and turquoise on his Western string tie was exquisitely done. His forehead was broad, his brown hair thinning, his approach and demeanor equally businesslike.

He smiled and stuck out his hand. "Sean Baldwin?" he asked, then introduced himself. "John Harvey. Please. Come with me." He turned away and walked toward the Bronco, leaving them to follow.

Behind them the pilot brought his engine back up to speed in a deafening roar and began to taxi down the highway. Sean's gaze swept the area.

Abbie walked behind and slightly to his side.

Harvey offered Sean the keys, explaining that if they would drop him back into town, they could take the four-wheel drive for their own use. He opened one of the back passenger doors and began to get in.

"Wait." Sean stopped him. The air was bitterly cold. The sunlight bouncing off the vast expanse of snow was blinding, but he'd spotted tracks in the snow he didn't like at all, at the borrow pit on the other side of the road, a hundred yards back. The hairs on the back of his neck rose.

Harvey looked over his shoulder.

"Are you armed?"

"Careful," Harvey commented amiably, nodding toward the gun rack mounted above the windshield. "I admire that."

"Is that all?"

"Well, no sir. Now that you mention it, that isn't quite all." Backing out, Harvey had to duck to clear the door frame. He turned and rose to his full height, then held up a hand to shade his eyes and looked in the direction of the tracks that had set off alarms in Sean's head.

The figure of a man rose up into view with a high-powered rifle at his shoulder and Sean knew beyond any doubt that it was Abbie's slender form in the cross hairs of the rifle scope.

Chapter Fifteen

Deeply angered, cursing himself, he told Abbie not to move.

Harvey smiled faintly. "Wise advice. Something more to admire. Now, perhaps you would be good enough to raise your own hands over your head so I can relieve you of your sidearm."

He did exactly as he was told. Abbie would buy a rifle slug in the back if he didn't. Harvey went directly to Sean's left side and took out his gun, then turned it on him. "Now, Ms. Callahan, get in the front passenger seat, and you, Mr. Baldwin, will still drive."

Sean couldn't believe this was happening. He hadn't begun to imagine a scenario in which Rorabaugh or Olivia Cameron could command this kind of ambush. What it told him was that Olivia was still very much in charge of her escape.

He didn't believe Harvey would pull the trigger. It would be simply too stupid to contemplate to kill for the sake of a woman fleeing her deadly husband—unless Olivia had convinced Harvey that Sean had been sent by her husband to kill her.

It ran through his mind that it wasn't that unlikely, that had he been in Harvey's shoes, seeing through Harvey's eyes an armed stranger fly into his backwater little town with a woman to double for the one he intended to kill, Sean might have bought the story, too.

But Harvey wasn't talking, and the gun trained at Abbie's head was loaded. Sean drove in the direction the Ford Bronco had been parked.

Abbie sat stiffly in the passenger seat to his right, her hands clasped tightly in her lap. She hadn't uttered a single sound, only followed directions exactly as they were given her. He sensed a level of quiet confidence in him coming from her that he couldn't believe and didn't deserve.

If he got them out of this at all, it would be pure damned dumb luck.

TWENTY MINUTES LATER—Abbie had nothing better to do than to watch the digital LED in the dashboard of the truck, certainly nothing else to keep her mind off Sean's gun pointed at the back of her head—he pulled into the circle drive of an enormous two-story ranch house. Built so that the back of the house had a view to the narrow, winding river, the house had several chimneys, smoke coming from three of them.

She wasn't, somehow, afraid. Her heart had slammed hard when Sean saw whatever it was he'd seen to make him so violently angry. When he'd told her not to move, she'd known her life hung in the balance, that she'd somehow gotten herself in the line of fire. Otherwise, Sean would never have been taken.

She trusted him implicitly. The fact that they had not been shot and dumped into some ravine ten feet deep in the snow and left for some winter-hungry predators to drag off and consume meant they still had a chance. She'd come to the conclusion she was certain Sean had already reached, as well. Olivia was still in the driver's seat, but she must fear they'd been sent to finish her off, or take her back to Charles Cameron, which had to be the same thing in her mind.

Harvey ordered Sean to keep his hands on the steering wheel and Abbie to get out of the truck. She got out. He kept Sean's gun trained on her up the porch steps. Her loafers squeaked on the hard layer of snow and ice.

When she had reached the door, Harvey called back to Sean. "Get out and follow her inside."

Sean did as he was told, as well. When he got near her he put his right hand at the small of her back and opened the door for her with his left.

"Over there," Harvey directed, following them inside, into a great room overflowing with old furniture and antiques. A fire crackled in the enormous granite fireplace that took up one entire wall.

The hardwood floor was stained a dark, rich color. Heavy beams crossed the high ceiling at ten foot intervals. Abbie tried not to look at the trophy heads mounted on the walls, but they were everywhere. A bighorn sheep, a buffalo, deer, antelope, a twelve-point elk, even trout of varying size and species mounted on display boards. Clearly, John Harvey was a man comfortable with guns.

She went to the fire to warm her hands and sit on the hearth, and when she turned, her eyes met those of

Olivia Cameron. She sat tucked deep in the corner of an oversize sofa facing the fireplace, looking as fragile, and more worn than Abbie could have imagined. The shadows beneath her eyes looked like bruises. She wore a wool plaid shirt and her signature leggings, but she seemed lost in her own clothes. Her beloved Sachi lay asleep next to her on the sofa.

Abbie's gaze darted to Sean, who must have seen Olivia in the same moment, then to John Harvey, leaning against a gun case fifteen feet from them, still training Sean's gun at the middle of her chest.

"You've met John," Olivia said. She turned her glance to him. "It's all right, now. I think you can put the gun away." Her host acceded to her wishes, setting the weapon aside.

"Where is Rorabaugh?" Sean asked.

"He'll be here shortly," Harvey replied, managing to convey without saying as much that it had been Rorabaugh with the rifle out on the highway.

Olivia trembled. "He sent you here, didn't he? To bring me back."

"Your husband?" Abbie asked gently.

"Yes. My... husband. Who else?" Fighting tears, she clamped her lips shut. Her chin puckered.

"No." Abbie exchanged glances with Sean. "He wanted us to find you, that much is true, but he doesn't know we're here. We—Sean and I—were nearly killed by a car bomb a couple of nights ago."

"Oh, my God! When is this ever going to stop?" she cried, clutching her middle. "He tried to *kill* you?"

"We don't know that, Olivia," Sean said, "but we haven't been in contact with him since."

"You don't know that?" she asked incredulously. "Do you have other enemies who would do such a thing, Mr. Baldwin?"

"None that I know of."

Abbie explained. "We don't know how it would serve his purposes, Olivia. He wanted us to find you. Why would he try to murder us?"

She shook her head in despair. "You would have to ask Charles. He doesn't need a reason. He's above that, you know."

"I don't know," Abbie objected as inoffensively as she could. "I know a lot of things about your husband that I didn't know before. I know he is capable of terrible things and that he lies to suit his purposes, but I don't know why he would try to kill us."

Olivia started to say something, then fell silent, curling tighter. Her jaw clenched and she wiped at tears on her mottled, pale cheeks. "If you know what he's capable of, then you know why he had to get rid of you.

"He k-killed my brother, you know?" she went on. "He destroyed Hal Gracie. He kept me drugged on painkillers for months on end after I left the hospital. He hired you to be me," she railed, her voice going higher, thinner. "And you, Mr. Baldwin, to protect me against a threat he manufactured. He ordered that h-hideous stone wall to be built, but it was a prison wall, you know? Meant to keep me in, meant to keep me home, meant to keep me from leaving him, even believing that I was going mad! If you know all this," she cried, "why isn't it obvious that he had to kill you, too?"

A man Abbie assumed must be Kenny Rorabaugh walked in then and dropped a set of keys into a metal dish on the sofa table behind Olivia. She jumped up and fled into his arms.

Only a few inches taller than Olivia, stockily built, he held her tight and stared defiantly at Sean, and then at Abbie from odd, angry, amber-colored eyes. John Harvey still stood leaning against the gun case, the strong, silent type.

"You know why, Livi," Rorabaugh said as much to Sean and Abbie as to the trembling, terrified woman in his arms. "Everyone always believes Charles Cameron."

Olivia pulled back. She covered her lips with the tips of her fingers for a moment, trying to collect herself. She breathed shallowly, then a little deeper, and pulled Rorabaugh with her to sit on the sofa again. "I want you to understand *me*. I want someone to understand."

Abbie did understand. She was as guilty as the rest of the world in believing Charles Cameron walked on water, in believing whatever he chose to reveal. And it was true that once she and Sean knew him for a liar—and in all likelihood, a murderer—Cameron would have had all the reason he needed to kill them, as well.

She also knew Olivia had spent years devoting herself to other people's children, to restoring them to their homes and families only to have her own baby bleed out of her body, her own brother murdered and her lover destroyed.

What Abbie couldn't understand was why Mitch Tensley was dead. Sean asked the question in the same moment she thought of it.

"What about Mitch Tensley?"

Olivia's head straightened on her shoulders. Fresh tears welled in her eyes. "What about him? He was my jailer."

A deep anger reached Sean's eyes. "He was my friend."

She bowed her head. "I'm sorry. I didn't mean that. I know he had two little boys. I would like to help them if I can."

Abbie thought her apology didn't do much to ease Sean's anger. "Olivia, if there was no one out there trying to kill you," Abbie asked softly, "why is Mitch dead?"

She picked at a jagged thumbnail. "Charles had already fired Kenny for talking too much to me."

"Cameron told us you two were in bed."

She turned her glance to Rorabaugh, then to Abbie. "It doesn't matter."

"It mattered to your husband," Sean said. "Didn't you think it might push him too far?"

"I didn't care."

Sean exhaled sharply. "Go on."

"I didn't know if I'd ever see Kenny again. I didn't know anything. I thought I had convinced Kenny to help me get out somehow, but then he was gone and Mitch came. I thought I had to start over with him, trying to make him believe me."

"What happened then?" Abbie asked.

Olivia clung to Rorabaugh's hands. "The day Mitch was killed, Charles had commanded me to stop talking to him. I believed I had only one last chance. I walked down to the river with him, just like I had every day. That was as far as Charles would consent to let me 'exert' myself.

"That day," she went on, ignoring tears spilling onto her wool plaid, "Charles was prepared to up the ante."

There *was* no end, Abbie thought, to Charles Cameron's acts of terrorism against his wife. Olivia confirmed what Abbie had seen coming.

"He'd fired Kenny, but that wasn't enough to make me behave and keep my mouth shut about him. The only way I was going to learn was if Mitch Tensley died. I don't think Charles would have minded very much at all then, if I'd been killed, too."

"The outpouring of public sympathy," Abbie mused.

"Yes. Poor Charles."

"How did you two reconnect?" Sean asked.

Rorabaugh got up to get Olivia some tissues. They all waited on her. "Kenny thought of a way. He knew about the charity ball. He knew that was the one thing Charles *had* to let me keep up with. I would be calling there every day. I would speak almost daily to the hospitality chief at the Stanhope, of course. So one day when I called, Kenny was there."

Her tears welled up again. Stroking her hair, Rorabaugh took over. "I told Livi I would get her out that first day. We talked about how. Cameron was in complete control. I knew a lot about the estate, the security system, the traffic in and out of the house, but Livi was not allowed out of her suite, so we came up with this plan to make a run for it on the night of the ball."

"That's when Charles brought you home," she said to Abbie. "I wanted to die. It was if he was saying to me, *You see, Liv."* Her voice was a perfect imitation of Cameron's supercilious tone. *"You must truly behave or I will simply replace you."*

"I'm very sorry." In her mind, Abbie recalled the ambassador calling her a liar, telling her that her apologies meant less than nothing to him. "I worried about that."

Olivia's look was accusation enough. Abbie's worries hadn't stopped her serving Charles Cameron's appalling purposes.

Abbie sensed Sean's anger billowing inside him again. She wanted to answer for herself. "Your husband's motives have nothing to do with mine in taking the job. I was warned that in taking your place, I would be drawing the threats on your life to me. I didn't think I'd be some sacrificial little lamb. I knew I would have a bodyguard, but it was always a possibility that whoever wanted you dead would get me instead."

After a look at the faces of her listeners, Abbie stopped trying to explain. It all sounded so pompous and overweening. She wasn't reaching Olivia anyway. Abbie understood why—Olivia knew there were never any threats against her life but the ones her husband manufactured. But she was also so wrapped up in herself that she couldn't begin to see that Abbie and Sean had been used, too.

"Anyway. You must ultimately have come up with a plan to leave the night of the charity ball."

Olivia's chin went up. "Yes. It was better than I could have imagined. You were with Charles, pretending to be me."

"Who threw the breaker on the camera circuit?" Sean asked Rorabaugh.

"Livi's maid, Jessica Sagermeyer."

Abbie nodded. "Of course. When she went to get the ballgown."

"The gate is on the same circuit. I scaled the wall and cracked the gate, then wired it so it looked like the electrical circuit was unbroken. Livi waited to come out until I called in on a cell phone patched through the Stanhope switchboards."

"After security had made the nine o'clock pass?" Sean asked.

Rorabaugh nodded. "We went down to the boat launch, I rowed down the river a couple miles, and we were home free."

Olivia seemed to grow more and more impatient with them all. She cut in when Rorabaugh would have gone on explaining. "I want you," she said, including Abbie and Sean in her sweeping look, "to go back and make him think I'm dead. I won't ever be free unless he believes I'm dead."

"Livi," Rorabaugh said, "it's not going to work. He will not believe you are dead unless he sees it for himself."

Olivia Simons Cameron shook her head. "No. He's got to believe it. Somebody has to make him believe it!"

"Olivia," Abbie said, "he's right. Charles Cameron will never accept that you're dead without real proof. Don't you see this is what he's hoping for? That you'll make some desperate mistake?"

"Like what?"

"Like having your father wire money here. It may go unnoticed, but why take the risk?"

Olivia stared at Abbie. Her tears had dried, but it was as if she simply had no more to shed. "I did it," she said, her voice little more than a whisper, "hoping that you would come. Please, Abbie. You've got to help me."

SHE ASKED Abbie to walk down to the river with her. She wanted to talk, *needed* to talk to another woman.

Sean objected. "Stay here and talk, Mrs. Cameron. Use the front porch, the back porch, the kitchen. You'll have all the privacy you need."

Abbie put her hand on his arm. "It's all right, Sean. I could use a walk myself."

"You can see every step of the way down to the river," Rorabaugh offered.

Sean looked at Rorabaugh, then Charles Cameron's desperate wife. "You won't mind if I make sure you're unarmed."

Olivia shook her head. "Of course not."

"And you understand that if anything, *anything* happens to Abbie, you won't make it out of here alive?"

"Sean—"

"Please. Abbie. Don't worry. It's okay. He should ask those things. We…we didn't exactly give you any reason to trust us when you flew in. I'm sorry for that. I wanted you to come, but…just like you, we had to be sure what your intentions were. Mr. Baldwin, you're very good. I understand you completely. Please."

She and Kenny Rorabaugh rose together. She walked to the center of the room and spread her arms. Abbie watched Sean pat her down. He ran his hands down the length of her body on both sides, up her legs, her breasts, the small of her back.

Rorabaugh's jaw tightened. "Should I make sure Abbie isn't armed, either?"

"That isn't necessary, Kenny," Olivia said. "If she had been armed, she had plenty of opportunity in the Bronco to pull a gun on John."

The owner of the guest ranch had remained silent all this time, just listening, shaking his head, Abbie thought almost certainly numbed by the kinds of things he'd heard. He was a man who understood sport and recreation, even the harsh reality in the wild of the survival of the fittest, but he didn't understand much of this.

He walked out of the front room ahead of them to an enormous coat closet. Pulling out Olivia's coat, he handed it wordlessly to Sean to check for weapons, then offered Abbie a pair of boots and a heavier coat.

Sean took Abbie out on the porch by himself. The late afternoon sun still shone fiercely off the snow. It was cold enough that their breath formed little puffs of frozen moisture. "You don't need to do this, Abbie. There is nothing she shouldn't be able to say to anyone. You don't owe Olivia Cameron anything."

"I know." She held out her hands to him, and he took them. "I'm not even sure that I trust her, but I want to do this. We've listened to Cameron's side of it for so long we don't even know what else there is."

Olivia stepped outside. Sean stepped back. By his look, Abbie knew Olivia understood herself to be warned again.

She descended the stairs and began trudging through the snow beyond an enormous pile of firewood, chopped and stacked against the house. Abbie tucked her hands into the pockets of the parka Harvey had loaned her and fell into step with Olivia, both of them kicking through snow.

At the back of the house Abbie could see the river still breaking through clumps of snow. She looked back up at the house, to a deck where Sean stood coatless and leaning against the railing, watching their progress.

She waved at him. He waved back. She turned to keep pace with Olivia.

She stopped a moment. "You're very much in love with Sean Baldwin, aren't you?"

Surprised that Olivia was not so self-involved that she hadn't noticed anything else, Abbie stared at her. She looked every one of her years in the brutal sunlight. Sad and still lovely, but aging. She looked away, down toward the river. "I am. Yes."

"Does he know?"

Abbie laughed softly. "Sean knows everything. Just ask him."

"Does he know, Abbie?" Olivia Cameron repeated.

She drew a deep breath. "No. I don't think he does."

Olivia gave a smile, a bittersweet smile women share. "Then he's not as smart as he thinks, is he?"

She started out again, picking her way around drifts that beneath the snow were small boulders.

She went so far as a fallen tree trunk, maybe fifteen or twenty feet from the river. This close, in all the awesome silence, the hurtling water seemed to roar.

Olivia swept at the snow piled on the tree trunk, making a place for them to sit. Abbie joined her. The scene on the river to the rear of the Cameron estate loomed suddenly in her mind, of Olivia arguing with Mitch Tensley. How she must have escaped in the dark very near to that point with Kenny Rorabaugh. A chill deeper than the mountain air went through her.

"Olivia, what is it?"

The older woman whom Abbie resembled so closely also shuddered. "Did you know the cell phone in my purse was something Charles knew nothing about?"

The chill inside Abbie went deeper. "No."

"I didn't think so."

"Why does it matter?"

"Abbie. It matters."

"I don't understand." But then she did. "Oh, my God. Olivia, no."

She buried her hands beneath her arms. "Yes. I, uh... I'm not proud of it, Abbie. All my life I've wanted children. Charles is impotent you know." She went on as if she had only just mentioned that her husband of fifteen years was left-handed or near-sighted or prone to burning too easily in the sun. "He's always blamed me for that. He says I intimidate him."

The cold inside Abbie seemed to have frozen her mind, numbed her reflexes. Olivia was first admitting, Abbie thought, that she was responsible for the

car bombing, and then dropping like another bomb-
shell the fact that her husband was impotent.

"Olivia, are you telling me you're the one who
placed the calls to your own cell phone?"

"Not me, but someone I know." One shoulder
shrugged upward. "Someone who needed to know
where you were, where the car could be found." She
turned to face Abbie. "I only meant to make Charles
understand me, that I could be as brutal as he was.
That if he wanted to up the ante, I would answer in
kind. He murdered Mitch Tensley. I was not above
arranging your death. You see how very desperate I've
grown. It didn't even matter to me that you would die,
if he would get the message."

Abbie clamped her fist over her mouth. Olivia Simons Cameron was quite mad, and though her logic
was tortured and insane, Abbie understood why she
had spoken at all of Charles Cameron's impotence. He
had put Olivia on such a pedestal that he could not
perform with her. The only way he would ever be able
to make love to his wife was if he could somehow, in
some way, reduce her to something less.

Other men, many of them, had taken her to their
beds, but that could only have made him feel still more
inadequate to her.

She stood. "Don't let him win, Olivia. Don't become what he is. Don't let him drag you down to this.
You've done so much in your life, so many things to
make a difference in the world."

But Olivia was shaking her head. "It's far too late,
Abbie. I have become the creature he molded, his
equal in transgressions. A woman he could touch

without failing." She gave a bitter laugh. "The irony is, I'm no longer the one he wanted."

Olivia drew a deep breath and bent as if to straighten her boot, but in her hand, when she straightened, was a small gun dusted with snow, surely no less deadly for the pristine white powder glittering like diamonds in the sun. She must have hidden it there hours ago, knowing she would bring Abbie here.

In a surreal way Abbie thought of her dad, of her promises every night to him, to be a good girl, and brave, and to stand up for what was right. She thought of her friend Bibi, and the tiny little girl with spina bifida.

Mostly she thought of Sean, what he meant to her; how even today, he had been right, and she'd been wrong to go for a walk with a crazy woman. She hoped Olivia was wrong, too, that Sean knew what he knew, which was that she loved him.

She wouldn't say die. She would not be so wrong as to give up. "Olivia, please. You don't have to do this. You've done nothing that can't be undone—"

"I'm truly sorry, Abbie, because you're young and in love, but I am what I have become to survive. I'm leaving the country. I have to go now, but when your body is shown to him, Charles will somehow manage to convince himself that it is me. Believing I am dead is the only way he will survive."

She stood, careful to keep the gun in her hand concealed from the view of the house. But when she would have had Abbie move on, a terrible, keening cry came from high above them on a bluff rising out of the riverbed like a mighty fist.

"Liiivv!"

She looked up on the bluff at Charles Cameron with a stark and soundless mask of terror. In a terrible slow-motion moment, Abbie turned, saw his rifle aimed at Olivia, and threw herself like her daddy had into the line of deadly fire.

And then Charles Cameron turned the rifle to his own chest and activated the trigger again, and dropped dead in his own merciless tracks.

THE AIRLIFT CHOPPER out of Denver transported Abbie to a trauma hospital, but what the emergency doctors called the Golden Hour, that critical time period in which a life is saved if it's going to be saved at all, had expired by the time they arrived. By the time Sean got to her, the snow had turned scarlet with her blood.

Charles Cameron was dead. Olivia's hound, Sachi, who had bolted the house when the shots were fired, cried and yapped and whined, but her mistress was catatonic, unable to respond to so simple a stimulus as her dog's cries. Cameron's shot had hit Abbie, but Olivia paid with her sanity.

As in all flight cases, Sean was left behind to follow in whatever manner he could find. John Harvey had the pilot who had brought them to Saratoga back in under an hour from the time the helicopter took off. The flight to Denver was the longest span of time Sean would ever know.

In his mind he relived the moment when he knew, when the scene on the surveillance video in which Mitch Tensley died merged with the action in the snow three hundred yards from where he stood. Afraid that Abbie would die, his heart thundered and his blood roared in his ears and his own cry sundered the still, frozen air.

The surgeons worked for sixteen hours, made an incision in Abbie's back twenty-three inches long, and used up forty-seven units of blood and plasma and platelets.

Abbie went through seventy-two hours in the critical care bed, and this morning, ten days after Thanksgiving, marked her seventh day in a coma from which she had yet to wake.

Her condition was referred to as "stable but guarded." The doctors had no physiological reason to give Sean for her continued coma.

Had any of Abbie's doctors been called upon to judge his condition, the term "unstable" would have come up. It took a bruiser the size and emotional weight of Dex Johnson to get him out of her room for a shower and a couple hours of sleep.

His many friends had come and gone, called and sent flowers and watched over her with him. But when they were all gone home, there was still Abbie, and Sean finally figured it out.

He loved her more than any hundred of his friends put together, which was saying a great deal. What it told him was that he could not live without her, at least not the life he wanted to live, and that he refused to let her go.

He wasn't into sissy gestures, he told himself, and he could not remember the last time he had cried. But he sat at her bedside and began to get truly furious, angry and afraid enough to tell her he loved her and she had no bloody business lying there ignoring him. His eyes brimmed with tears for resenting her shabby treatment. "You picked one fine damned time to be right, Abbie," he railed.

He thought he heard her whispering but refused to look because too many times the gentle hiss of the respirator had fooled him into thinking he heard her soft whisper. But while he was avoiding looking toward her pale, beautiful face so he wouldn't be disappointed again, her hand moved toward his.

His throat tightened till he thought he couldn't breathe. He turned, and saw her eyes open, the shadow of a smile, the effort at breathing. It took her a full half minute to get it out, but she finally managed. "To be right about what?"

He knuckled a tear away before one could actually spill. "You saved Olivia's life, Abbie."

"Will she be . . . okay?"

Sean nodded. "She's free, Abbie. She'll be okay. It may take years of therapy, but she'll be okay." He hesitated. His voice hardly worked. "You were damned well supposed to leave handling the speeding bullets routine to me."

Abbie's eyes fluttered closed. Pleasure swamped her heart.

He would stop speeding bullets for her, and she knew what that meant—it was better in all the world than if he'd said aloud that he loved her.

HARLEQUIN®

I N T R I G U E ®

In steamy New Orleans, three women witnessed the same crime, testified against the same man and were then swept into the Witness Protection Program. But now, there's new evidence. These three women are about to come out of hiding—and find both danger and desire....

eye WITNESS

Start your new year right with all the books in the exciting EYEWITNESS miniseries:

#399 A CHRISTMAS KISS
by Caroline Burnes (December)

#402 A NEW YEAR'S CONVICTION
by Cassie Miles (January)

#406 A VALENTINE HOSTAGE
by Dawn Stewardson (February)

Don't miss these three books—or miss out on all the passion and drama of the crime of the century!

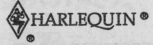

The collection of the year!
NEW YORK TIMES BESTSELLING AUTHORS

Linda Lael Miller
Wild About Harry

Janet Dailey
Sweet Promise

Elizabeth Lowell
Reckless Love

Penny Jordan
Love's Choices

and featuring
Nora Roberts
The Calhoun Women

This special trade-size edition features four of the wildly popular titles in the Calhoun miniseries together in one volume—a true collector's item!

Pick up these great authors and a chance to win a weekend for two in New York City at the Marriott Marquis Hotel on Broadway! We'll pay for your flight, your hotel—even a Broadway show!

Available in December at your favorite retail outlet.

NEW YORK
Marriott®
MARQUIS

HARLEQUIN®   Silhouette®

NYT1296-R

As Seen on TV!

Free Gift Offer

With a Free Gift proof-of-purchase from any Harlequin® book, you can receive a beautiful cubic zirconia pendant.

This stunning marquise-shaped stone is a genuine cubic zirconia—accented by an 18" gold tone necklace. (Approximate retail value $19.95)

Send for yours today...

compliments of ⬧HARLEQUIN®

To receive your free gift, a cubic zirconia pendant, send us one original proof-of-purchase, photocopies not accepted, from the back of any Harlequin Romance®, Harlequin Presents®, Harlequin Temptation®, Harlequin Superromance®, Harlequin Intrigue®, Harlequin American Romance®, or Harlequin Historicals® title available in August, September or October at your favorite retail outlet, together with the Free Gift Certificate, plus a check or money order for $1.65 U.S./$2.15 CAN. (do not send cash) to cover postage and handling, payable to Harlequin Free Gift Offer. We will send you the specified gift. Allow 6 to 8 weeks for delivery. Offer good until December 31, 1996, or while quantities last. Offer valid in the U.S. and Canada only.

Free Gift Certificate

Name: _____

Address: _____

City: _____ State/Province: _____ Zip/Postal Code: _____

Mail this certificate, one proof-of-purchase and a check or money order for postage and handling to: HARLEQUIN FREE GIFT OFFER 1996. In the U.S.: 3010 Walden Avenue, P.O. Box 9071, Buffalo NY 14269-9057. In Canada: P.O. Box 604, Fort Erie, Ontario L2Z 5X3.

FREE GIFT OFFER   084-KMFR
ONE PROOF-OF-PURCHASE
To collect your fabulous FREE GIFT, a cubic zirconia pendant, you must include this original proof-of-purchase for each gift with the properly completed Free Gift Certificate.

084-KMFR

You are cordially invited to a

HOMETOWN REUNION

September 1996—August 1997

Where can you find romance and adventure
bad boys, cowboys, babies. Feuding families,
arson, mistaken identity, a mom on the run…?
Tyler, Wisconsin, that's where!

So join us in this not-so-sleepy little town and
experience the love, the laughter and the
tears of those who call it home.

WELCOME TO A
HOMETOWN REUNION

As if the arson investigator hadn't stirred up
enough talk in Tyler, suddenly wigwams are
cropping up around Timberlake Lodge. And
that gorgeous "Chief Blackhawk" is taking
Sheila Lawson hostage, without even knowing
he's doing it. *Hero in Disguise,* the fourth
in a series you won't want to end….

**Available in December 1996
at your favorite retail store.**

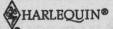

HTR4

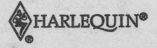